Narcissistic
Praise-Junkies

Angie Bennett

DEDICATION

For my Settlement Home girls

1

"Godsmack!"

"That's a good one," I answered, glancing at Twitch briefly. "But it's gobsmacked."

"Monkeyballs," he said dispassionately.

"Not real. So you better mean the juggling kind." Trixie giggled at him with a timbre in her voice.

"I got it off urbanslang.com."

"Monkeyballs? You needed a dictionary for that? That's not what I had in mind for vocabulary development."

"No. Godsmack. Godsmack!" he said real, this time. Then, "God! Smack. Godsmack," he finished with a bleat, zoo sounds.

"It's gobsmack. Gobsmacked, really." I corrected, exaggerating the B and launching a miniscule dot of saliva unto Munch's history mind map. "Try

zounds, again. That worked for a while."
More zoo sounds.

"What's that?" Munch asked, and I feared that he was going to chastise me for my spittle on his project, which I couldn't allow, and then there would be his saliva and possibly a chair flying into my face. "Zounds. Sounds like Scooby-Doo," he laughed his cartoon laugh.

"I think that was zoiks or zoinks," I said absorbing the saliva dot with the cuff of my blouse. Munch laughed again. His name was Austin, but in my head I called him Munch; actually, in my head I called him worse than that, but Munchhausen by Proxy was my unofficial diagnosis of his craziness. "It's short for 'God's wounds,'" I told him. "Finish your mind map," I tapped his largely blank poster board, a faithful map of his mind I was sure. No wonder his mother had convinced so many of his fictional traumatic brain injury. "People said zounds to keep from cursing, using God's name in vain. Like gosh." I had tried from the beginning to eliminate the cursing. I had gotten pretty creative.

"What else goes in the French Revolution?" I prompted. He had only a misspelled title and a pile of severed heads in the corner and a guillotine that looked like he had drawn it with his toes. I wanted him to produce something besides a pile of headless torsos, which he would, given enough time. When his world history teacher gave him an A-plus, I wanted him to have at least tried to earn it. His teacher had reported to me that Munch would get an A for every day the "fat retard" stayed out of his classroom, stayed in the unit with me. I couldn't blame him. "Are these the heads of rich people or poor people? Criminals?" I suggested. "Who was being guillotined?"

Jacky clacked her calculator closed and rolled out of her desk. "I can lick my own," she looked around the room and smiled at Trixie, "...armpit," she announced, as if she'd been saving this up until she'd finished her consumer math to the best of her ability. "Can you lick yours?" She paused, too long. "Armpit, I mean? Do you shave, Trixie?"

"Of course," Trixie said and looked away, out the window. I could tell it was something else she'd forgotten. I thought maybe I should write a book for girls like Trixie. *How to Become a Real Live Girl.*

Jacky straddled a chair facing the reading corner where the freshmen were working, stretched her arms over her head, leaned back like a cat in a field of freshly sprouted catnip, her unrestrained breasts aggressively stretching her tank top, and tucked her face to the side,

7

ridging her tongue along the track of tendon inside the curve of her armpit.

"That's enough, Jacky," I said, but I'd waited too late. I'd been curious to see if she could. And why she thought it would be a good idea.

"Zounds!" Trevor yelled, his eyes crossing and uncrossing in full head-flopping tic.

"Zounds," Austin mocked. "Zoiks!"

"Sorry, Miss," Jacky sounded contrite, but did not change her posture. She must have learned this on her porn shoot summer job. That's the essay she'd written last week, her What-I-Did-for-Summer-Vacation essay. A Day as a Porn Star. She'd called it the money shot—lick your armpit. Jacky raised herself to her feet effortlessly and walked back to her desk, saying not-quietly-enough, "What ya' got there, Trixie?" Stage whisper, another porn movie lesson. She threw her head back and mimed masturbating a penis. Why all the tossed heads? Did people really do that when they were having sex?

"Bitch," Trixie whispered, truly whispered, tearing, turning in her seat, though I don't think we could have seen her erection with the pleats in her skirt. But Twitch was trying hard to catch a glimpse.

"Motherflapper! Pigeon, pigeons. Flapping pigeon-flapper," Twitch's tic overtook him. Bless him. Pigeons. He was trying.

"It's SSR time," Booger said to his freshmen classmates without lifting his eyes from his book. "*Silent. Sustained. Reading.* No one is reading. You're not silent, Trevor," he said to Twitch. "And you're not sustaining anything except my frustration level," he said to Trixie.

"Oh, she is, and I'll give you something to sustain too, Nathan," Jacky purred.

"That doesn't even make any sense," Booger protested, but then, in his TV commercial lawyer voice, "If you sustain an erection for longer than four hours, please call your doctor. Dr. Jacky? Hello?" he said, never looking away from Heinlein's *Have Spacesuit will Travel.* Nathan's Asperger's syndrome made him an easy target, but he was witty enough to defend himself when he needed to.

"Freshmen, fill out your reading logs. Jacky, it's almost time for government. Austin, how about some headless corpses in fancy clothes for this mindmap?" It was only seconds away from the bell, and I had to get these kids launched. I had an appointment.

The kids awakened from their hormone fog. The Whale, snoring in the middle of the floor, was not even aware of Jacky's obscene show. And he'd be sorry to have missed it. I nudged The Whale's foot with my yard stick. If I used my foot, he'd accuse me of kicking him, and his mother would plant herself firmly between my butt cheeks. Of course, I guess this could qualify as hitting him with a stick. "Don't forget to come back here for lunch. No free lunch tickets today; we are having Mr. Humphrey's going away party. Did everyone sign the card?" I asked but was cut off by Mr. Humphrey's entrance.

"Alrighty. Y'all ready? Whale! Get up from there. This ain't kindey-garden. There's no naptime." He snapped his runner against The Whale's calf-high lace-up steel-toed combat boot. Since it was Mr. H.'s last day, I wished he'd kicked him harder. And in the face, God forgive me. "You stay here, you going to get a demerit. No pizza party for you."

The Whale rolled over, pulled his Guitar Hero t-shirt over his ample gut and got up on his knees. "I'm going."

"Geography, boys," Mr. H. said to Trevor, Nathan, and The Whale; then to Trixie, "and my lady."

The four freshmen lined up and obediently trekked out behind Mr. Humphrey. The sophomores, Munch and The Count, did not need to be escorted this year. So far. Becca's OCD might make them tardy, but it would keep them out of trouble, and Munch was just stupid and horny enough to follow her everyday as she counted the lockers between the NP unit and geometry.

"Jacky, you going to make it? Or do I need to call the SRO?"

"Who's on duty? Officer Hotty?"

"If it were, I would not have given you the option."

"Oh, Officer Muff—"

"Jacky," I warned.

"Alright, I'm going." I picked up the phone to warn her teacher to expect her, and I walkied the officer to let her know that loose Jacky was on the loose, in case any young boys or lesbian transsexuals went missing.

This was my third year teaching in the behavior modification unit, what the administration called the NP unit, New Pathways. What I called the Narcissistic Praise-Junkie unit. Though it wasn't catchy—I mean it had been once but it was now cliché—it was at least descriptive. I'd borrowed it from the U.S. Navy back in 2007 when they'd called the MySpace generation a bunch of Narcissistic Praise-Junkies, but since the MySpace generation had faded into the Facebook generation, I had

11

appropriated it for my own eminent domain.

Humphrey had been in the unit from the time the school had decided that there were just some kids who needed a different place to go instead of the office. Someplace where they weren't "in trouble" but "got support." In reality, it just gave the administration time to do something besides see the same children over and over—and convinced the parents that the district was genuinely concerned about their delinquent, violent, or cannibalistic teenagers.

Of course they didn't, but the nut doesn't fall far from the tree so the parents believed the unit was not really a cell in the basement but a real room where someone cares. And at first, that was Humphrey, a tough but loved former bus driver with faltering eye sight.

The first year there was just the one kid. It was my senior year, and there had been a fire, supposedly set in a football player's locker. It spread. The kid, though, was "some kind of retard," one overly chatty teacher said, "so they couldn't just expel him," even though it was the third fire of the year, all having originated from some jock's backpack.

Now, Humphrey was retiring. Finally. There was a sheet cake in the teachers' lounge and the pizza would be delivered right before A-lunch. And that would be the only acknowledgment he got. The kids wouldn't miss him, and his replacement, if one could consider such a thing, would be a nice change of pace, I hoped.

My new assistant, Krista, had dropped out of a teacher education program after her second year when she had moved to the Austin area. She'd seemed nice at the interview, but not too nice. I'd already pegged her candy-coated voice as pure fraud, and I thought we would get along fine. Mostly I liked that she would take the job, and she'd been interested enough in teaching that she'd enrolled in college, which may also mean she could perhaps read and write.

I'd hoped she would be punctual also, but it was already about 2 minutes too late for that to happen. I'd scheduled her first orientation for the only 40 minutes of the day that I had to myself—usually to do paperwork, prepare for special education meetings, call parents, write lesson plans or grade papers—but which I usually spent praying fervently for self-control, patience, or an aneurism.

I thought that if she did, eventually, show up it would be nice if she saw me doing some work. I sat down at my desk, an odd thing in the middle of the day, and I already had 17 emails from my hemorrhoid parents: Munch Mom and Mama Whale. Most behavior unit kids, in my opinion, did not have a disability outside of their parents. Too much parenting or too little.

I was seven minutes into mom's epistolary account of Munch's soupy-poopy—"Could you keep an eye on that, please?"—when Krista peeked in the door.

"My God, it's like a maze to get up here," she said. She dropped her fake Louis Vuitton body bag onto my desk. "Where's the kids?" I corrected her grammar in my head.

"They are all in class for once. Well, for the last nine and a half minutes," I said coming around the desk to greet her.

"Oh, I thought they lived here," she said, and I was sure that I liked her—not because she was joking, but because she'd taken the job anyway, believing we spent the full work day with seven deranged teenagers.

"All of them are required to attend at least one of their scheduled classes, their out-classes, each day. Many of them attend all their classes, except when they get in trouble, and they only come here for social skills class, English, and check-in." I started in right away.

"We don't really have a lot of time, and I want to get you briefed as much as possible before the kids get here," I only minimally alluded to her tardiness. "If they know you are clueless, they will pull out your eyeballs and sell them on eBay as rare gelatinous earrings." I wasn't sure if the look on her face was her sarcasm meter, or her trying to determine the meaning of gelatinous.

"Okay, shoot," she said, scooting her purse aside to sit on my desk.

"We're going to need to lock up your purse. You'll have a key to the file cabinet on your key chain when I get it from Mr. Humphrey this afternoon." I pulled out my keys and crammed her plastic purse on top of mine in the bottom drawer. "We don't have any adjudicated thieves at the moment, but you never know. Okay let's start from the top. Jacky." I pointed to her binder on the top shelf above my desk. "You can find all the official documentation in there, but the real stuff is not there. She's seventeen. Suffering from DDH, but don't quote me on that."

"DDH? That's like ADHD or something?"

"Nope. Daddy did her." Krista gasped and then laughed. She needed to see right away that this job required some comic relief. The kids' problems were so big and bad, we couldn't do anything except extricate ourselves, usually through humor, but I had a whole toolbox of space-creating ploys. "As a result, she is trying to find real love, but she thinks she's only got one tool."

"Between her legs," Krista said. I was so glad we understood each other.

"So she acts out sexually," I elaborated, "as often and overtly as possible. That's the senior class. We have one junior right now, getting another one this week or next. This one, I call him The Whale and that's how he introduces himself so I just stick with it. He a big boy. Probably close to 300 pounds, and tall." Krista looked up at me. I was over six feet tall, so if I called him tall he would seem like a giant to her. "I don't think he belongs here; under normal parenting conditions just a FLK, funny-looking kid, but he's labeled 'other health impaired' because he's depressed. Took a bottle of ibuprofen a while back. I think it was just to get his parents' attention although I doubt he ever lacked for attention. You okay?"

"Scared, but good. Who else?" She was keeping pace with me; a good sign.

"New one next week. Junior, he says, but he's a home-school victim so we're not really sure, no credits to transfer in. He's in regular classes right now. That's all I know.

"Sophomores, there's Munch. His name's Austin. Never call him Munch. I call him Munch because he's a Munchhausen by Proxy kid—"

"Oh my God, how awful." She bit her lip, "What's that?"

"It means his mom hurts him to get sympathy. Happens with babies a lot. Really, I guess the kids don't live long enough to be teenage Munches very often. It's an interesting case. According to mom, he's got a traumatic brain injury, ADHD, epilepsy, inflammatory bowel syndrome, and ODD, which is oppositional defiant disorder—which means he's kind of a twit—and, geez, what else? Bi-polar, maybe?" The phone rang, an internal call, "Here we go," I told Krista hitting the speaker phone button. "Ellie Warden," I said toward the phone.

"Hey, it's Sanders. You need to come get Jason," he barked into the phone. Krista raised her eyebrows trying to evaluate if this was normal.

"Why? What'd she do?" I asked the coach. "Trixie," I told Krista.

"Are you kidding me? We've had this conversation every single day this year."

"It's only the second week of school, tell me again. I'm not that bright." I pressed the voice memos button on my iPhone to record the call. "Coach, be aware that my new instructional assistant is present."

"I don't give a good goddamn. You got to get this fairy out of my gym."

"Why, did she refuse to dress out?"

"She? That's bullshit. This is men's athletics. He is wearing a leotard and leg-warmers."

"Yeah, it is a little warm for leg warmers," I agreed. "You can send her up."

"She won't leave. He. Dammit."

"Put her on the phone," I said and Trixie came right on. I cringed to think she had heard his entire conversation.

"Sweetie, you're out of dress code. You'll get a dress code violation when you get back. That'll be demerits." I switched off the recorder.

"Okay. Sorry, Ms. Warden."

"Don't apologize to me; it's not my rule. You got the shorts I gave you?"

"Yes," Trixie said.

"So you were just being provoking."

"Provocative."

"Although I'm sure some of the boys secretly thought so, that's different. Either change or get your spandexed butt back up here." I hung up before the

18

coach could come back on. I turned to Krista, "Freshwoman. Transgendered. She's trying to make a statement. She's probably going to get herself hate-crimed."

"You going to get her?"

"No, it's too close to transition now. I've got to be here when the others come or they'll go wild, start robbing banks and eating monkeys."

"What will happen to her?"

"She'll be fine. She'll be here. There's pizza for lunch. And a cake. She may dress like a siren, and act like a vixen, but she eats like a man."

2

There's always a teacher's helper. Often a little brown-nosing sycophant that not even the teacher likes. Sends him on errands just to get the little beast out of her sight. I did not have one of those. Sending anyone of my little darlings out into the halls was like loosing a weapon of mass destruction—or at least mass frustration.

The only one who could be trusted without the "Incoming!" phone warning was the one I called Ass Booger, for his Asperger's syndrome, known as Booger—or Nathan by his family and friends, or would have been if he'd had any friends. He wasn't dangerous, except to himself, and not in a suicidal way. No chance. He was the smartest person he'd ever met. He loved himself, but he could irritate Mother Teresa into homicidal rage in about five minutes, which was really saying something since she had been dead for so long.

When the phone rang, I did a quick inventory of my seven dwarves: Sexy, Twitch, Munch, Tranny, The Whale, The Count, and Booger so it couldn't be someone asking me to come and talk one of them down from a ledge or manipulate them out of their hostages.

I hit the speaker phone button. "Pizza's here," the secretary announced.

"Thanks, I'll send someone down," I answered.

"Who?" I heard the tension in her voice. Panic almost. But I disconnected. It'll be a surprise, I thought. "Nathan, can you go get the pizza?"

"That's not fair. He always gets to go," Munch protested.

"He hasn't received a single demerit this week," I pointed out.

"I haven't gotten one today," he argued.

"The day is not over," I said. Then, "Okay, Austin, go help him with the pizza. The girls will go get the cake."

"When will Mr. Humpy be back?" The Count asked.

"Humphrey, Becca. Soon, so you better get going. There are a lot of open doors to count between here and the lounge," I told her, hoping that the

21

suggestion would hurry her along. There were a lot more lockers than open doors.

I watched Booger scurry to the door to hold it open for The Count and Jacky. They thanked him politely. My social skills training in the real world. I smiled. I liked my job, or at least it averaged out that way, I'd told Krista. Some days I loved it and about as many days I wanted to check myself into a mental ward, or volunteer to be a test subject for the new and only somewhat improved lobotomy, or maybe just give in and perform a DIY neutering on one of the little narcissistic praise-junkies so I could be on the front page of the *Austin American Statesman* and wouldn't have to come back. At least I was honest with myself about one thing, I loved the drama. And I loved feeling like I did something that very few people would do. Not could do; I really thought the job was easy enough with the right attitude and skill set, but I would not admit that except under torture because I was the worst praise-junkie of all. The most important tools in my coping kit were a punching bag and a fluffy cat. And a very occasional stolen cigarette.

My Maine coon kitty was my role model. She was intimidating, like me, mostly due to her size. She was a 30 pound cat and I was a woman who referred to herself as a dainty 5'14". Edna, though, was utterly cool—unflappable—and as forgiving as the Easter bunny. I tended to be more self-absorbed and about as giving as a wishing well. I hoped that the sacrament of reconciliation and the non-sacramental tithing provided parity.

Even with a daily endorphin-fueling workout and all the kitty-belly I could pet, tackling deranged children armed with staplers and caustic profanity was getting harder, and this was only the beginning of my third year. By retirement age I'd be the emotional equivalent of one of those leathery small town truck stop waitresses who had to put up with the constant demands of querulous patrons who treated the restaurant like a roadhouse bar.

That thought train reminded me to take out my camera. This was still a small town, and my mom had waited tables long enough to take an unnatural glee in her peers' psycho grandchildren, no matter how vaguely known to her those folks had been. And she swore that she knew Mr. Humphrey before he was allowed to eat at the lunch counter.

With some of the kids out fetching the food, I put The Whale, Trixie, and Twitch to work on the classroom.

"I'll do the streamers!" Trixie squealed enthusiastically, and I decided to have a heart to heart with her.

"Trixie, come talk to me. Krista, can you get the boys to put out the plates and napkins? And don't argue, Whale, if you want to eat, you're going to participate." Of course, I knew he wouldn't do any actual work. "Here, take some pictures for the scrapbook," I said, handing him my camera.

Trixie came to the sofa by the window. I'd carefully mapped a square in red tape around it after I'd found Jacky dry-humping one of my PTSD kids (profoundly-traumatized-screaming-demon) there last spring. No one entered the Red Square without permission from the dictator.

Indicating leave to enter and sit on the couch, I said, "Trix, do you remember the last words you said out loud?"

"Um, no ma'am. Did I curse?"

"No, not cursing. It had to do with the decorations?"

"Oh, the streamers," the squeal again.

"Trixie, girls over seven, or anyone who ever wants to have sex with a girl over seven, does not talk that way." I let that sink in. "Now, are you a man? Or are you a lesbian? Because those are the two options you've explored this school year. If the answer is yes to either of those questions, and I recognize that may change from one hour to the next, you cannot ever repeat the combination of decorating with that tone of voice."

"Yeah, kinda' faggy, huh?" Trixie answered in her real male voice.

"I need support in C Hall. Repeat, I need support in C Hall," the walkie crackled with Mr. White's tense voice. I looked at Krista. Could I leave her here with the three NP's?

"E.W. responding," I said into the walkie. "Let's go." I sounded a little too James Bond, but in my defense, I had no idea what was happening on the other side of the walkie. I got the fire drill rope from above the door. The fire drill rope was a ski rope about 12 feet long with rubber handles equi-spaced on each side. The handles were much too small for my kiddos. They were meant for primary grades, but I had more use for it than the average second grade teacher. I grabbed the centipede head and Krista the tail—she would be a good follower, I could tell—and we headed down the hall toward C stairwell.

"What's your location, E.W.?" the impatient principal prompted over the walkie at my waist. "Dammit," I said.

"Try 'zounds,'" Twitch said, which set him off, and he shouted halting suggestions into The Whale's ear all the way down the steps and down the hall to the atrium. I heard Jacky's of-course-I-will heels clicking and The Count numbering her steps behind me.

"Come on, girls, grab ahold, it's a rescue mission," I said. Krista took the cake from Becca.

"Who are we rescuing?" The Count asked.

"The principal, I think," I said.

———

If Mr. White had set down his coffee cup and plaque declaring us a Blue Ribbon School to pick up the walkie-talkie, it must be at least a minor felony. I could hear Nathan before I saw him, and I wondered if I should rename the dwarves making him The Howler instead of the more general Ass Booger. Before Asperger's had been assigned its more unfortunate name, it had been called the Little Professor's Syndrome due to its victims' didactic and unaware mien. The "teacher (or mom or—more rarely—coach) likes me best" disorder.

Nathan was awkwardly straddling Munch beside the trophy case, his skinny legs spread wide over the older boy's girth, Principal White stood benignly between my wrestling boys and his precious glass wall of basketball, tennis and Odyssey of the Mind trophies—which meant nothing in Texas where high school football was a religion.

Bellowing wildly, Booger was head-butting the chest and neck of his foe while aggressively protecting his sternum with his crossed arms.

"Nathan Michael Harmon," I said sternly, "I require that you stand on your feet and explain your actions." I couldn't allow him to use my lack of precise language as an excuse to disobey. The skinny, floppy-haired boy raised himself without removing his hands from his pits and stood before me. Munch, who had struggled only minimally before, began to wail and thrash.

"He was going to put my nipples on the pizza," Booger explained, as righteously indignant as one can manage with a snot faucet on one's face.

"Austin, what did you tell him," I asked, bending to put the pizzas back in their boxes. I saw the grease stains then on Munch's shirt, little circles. Nathan grabbed his handle on the fire drill rope but still curved protectively around his chest. "Austin, answer me. Did you tell Nathan that pepperonis were made

27

from nipples?" His writing and bawling morphed into laughing spasms.

"Boy nipples!" he roared.

"Get these freaks back to their cage, Ms. Warden," the principal said, straightening his tie as he retreated.

"I guess it's bologna sandwiches for us today," Jacky said and gave Nathan a sympathetic look I should have interpreted, should have intercepted, but before I could it was already done. "And you know where bologna comes from. Right, Nate?" She lifted up her thin shirt, exposing her breast; she drew a circle around her merely Canadian bacon, not bologna, sized areola.

The Whale, holding my camera all this time, snapped a photo and dropped the camera down his pants. Then the cake hit the floor and Becca followed it.

3

Manny's Camaro was parked under the live oak tree in Mama's front yard. Mama's motion activated recording of a barking dog arfed as my kitty came to greet me, nosing open the screen door. She leapt to the porch railing, then to my shoulders. "Mama?" Edna curled in closer around my neck as I shifted the paper grocery sack from arm to hip to open the door. She knew the bag would soon be hers, her favorite toy since she was a little kitten.

"We're in here, Ellie," Mom called from the kitchen. I wondered how often Manny showed up in my absence to eat the groceries I provided. "She's gonna' want something green," Mama said to my brother confidentially.

"I'm right here, Frances," I chided my mother.

"I know, sugar. You want me to open a can of something?"

"A can of whoop-ass, teacher?" Manny said.

"What are we having?"

"Barbeque weenies and macaroni and cheese," she said. This was not food I'd bought. Either Manny brought it himself or this is what Mama bought with her food stamps, which is what she still called her Lone Star Card, and brought out only for Manny because I would never sanction such dietary disasters. Mom may be able to get away with such choices. You can forgive a gnome for being fat—Mama was only 5'2"—but if you're a woman over six foot tall and fat, not to mention thirty-two and never married, people made assumptions, as my brother did not hesitate to point out. Manny was leaning against the cabinet, shirtless as usual.

"Is it a law that you have to drive a Camaro without a shirt on?" I asked.

"Only in Texas." My brother, and everyone else in town, loved to play up the ignorant redneck thing, even though we lived in an Austin suburb, the most liberal oasis in the state. The only liberal oasis in the state.

"Some green beans? Creamed spinach?" Mama asked, waving her can-opener.

"A beer?" Manny asked, "Mom bought it at the parish bake sale on Sunday."

"No, Mama, don't bother. I'll eat a salad." Edna jumped from my shoulders onto the kitchen table, and Manny snatched up his beer like she was going to lap it up. Beer was an almost non-existent treat at Mom's house because Manny wasn't sharing his beer, I wouldn't buy it, and Mom couldn't buy it with foodstamps. "You bought beer at a bake sale?"

"Yes, Father Nugent brought it. He said he doesn't bake."

"It's Father Nguyen," I corrected.

"Get that cat off my table. He's getting hair in everything."

"It's a girl, Mom."

"That monster is too big to be a girl."

"You mean me or the cat, Mom?"

Edna was a thirteen year old Maine coon, named after the Maine poet, Edna St. Vincent Millay. I'd bought her my second year in college after declaring myself an English major. I figured having a 30 pound cat was about as useful as a degree in English. Of course, at the time I didn't think that way; I thought that I would be a famous novelist, but I may as well earn a degree, in case I ever had to get a real job. Because nothing helps you get a real job like a liberal arts degree. Mom lifted Edna off the table and cooed to her as she lowered her to the floor. She only pretended to be annoyed by the cat when Manny was around.

"How's school?" Mama asked, opening a can of green beans.

"Well, today we had what shall forever be known as the Nipple Riot. No one was arrested or hospitalized, unfortunately."

"Did I tell you that Tiffany had a miscarriage?" Manny said, "speaking of hospitals, I mean."

"Who's Tiffany?" I asked.

"Well now she's gonna' be my ex-girlfriend. Thank God."

"The Milk of Magnesia work, then?" Mom asked ladling bacon grease onto the flaccid green beans.

"Yeah, among other things," Manny said.

"What other things, son?"

"You don't want to know that, Mom." He leered at me, like I might know what illicit things one would do to induce a miscarriage in a girl not yet able to vote.

"Why don't you just use a condom, Manny. God, how many times are we going to go through this?"

"I beg your pardon, miss, do not use the Lord's name in vain in my house, and we are Catholic, birth control is against our religion."

"A 26 year-old man impregnating a teenager is not?" I asked.

"Two wrongs don't make a right," Mama said.

I finished putting the groceries on the counter, leaving them out so Manny and Mama could observe the healthy food choices I had made. Whole wheat pasta, fresh fruit, actual green beans, organic yogurt. I turned the paper bags over to Edna.

"Age of consent, teacher," Manny said forking an amply cut wiener into his mouth.

"You should have taught your girlfriend to do that," I said.

"Teacher, teacher, can you teach me?" he sang before putting the wiener back between his lips, in and out and in again.

Manny referred to me as a teacher as often as possible, like a schoolyard taunt. He was a little envious of my college degree, and a little wary of my teacher status. I had started college when he started junior high, and when Mom was confronted with our conflicting work ethic, Manny began to look a little too much like Dad.

Plus my student teaching had been his junior English class, and he'd never forgiven me for explaining necrophilia as it related to William Faulkner's "A Rose for Emily" to the head cheerleader. I was probably the only student teacher ever to have the principal call her mom.

"Free at last, free at last," Manny said then chomped off a corner of his bread and chewed. "Oh, I'm having a miscarriage. Oh, ow," he said and spat the bite back onto his plate, pointing at it in case I'd missed his metaphor.

"Savage," I said, and Manny began to sing our high school fight song with a mouth full of masticated white bread and barbequed pig snouts and buttholes.

"We are the Savages strong and proud," he sang. Sauce dripped onto his chin, bloodlike, proving his point.

"Manny Warden," my mom bellowed, smacking at his shoulder with her dishtowel. I knew it was times like this that she regretted that she hadn't given him a middle name. Or even a real full first name. My blonde brother was no Manuel, after all. Mom said it had been Emmanuel which means "God with us," but after Daddy's death it had seemed sacrilegious.

He gave her an innocent grin. "My little gift from God and man," Mama said, scratching Manny behind the ear like a cat. Manny pretended to purr, spewing flecks of barbeque sauce onto the table cloth.

"So you didn't think about Hoovering Manny when you found out you were pregnant?" She hadn't even begun to show at Daddy's funeral.

"Eloise! I will not stand for that disrespect." If Mom was really going to lecture me, she'd need a smoke; she stopped her shouting at me long enough to light her cigarette.

"Hoover?" I mouthed at Manny while she was distracted. He cocked his head, raised his eyebrows and shoulders just a bit in a what's-a-guy-to-do gesture.

"How could you say such a thing? I am a good Catholic woman. Sure, I knew it was going to be hard to raise two kids on my own, with me never working before, then waiting tables until I couldn't no more."

"I know, Mom, I'm sorry," I said, clearing the dishes, balancing bowls on my arms just like Mama had taught me. I really was sorry, too. For having given mom another opportunity to be the commendation-seeking martyr. "It was really hard on you. I only meant to tease Manny, not be disrespectful." I had taught my students how to give a sincere sounding apology before arguing their case, and I gave myself lots of opportunities for practice.

"Abortion is nothing to joke about," Mom continued, but the fire was out of her now. I peeked inside the Thriftway bag at Edna, and she promptly threw herself backward to expose her belly for rubbing. What a slut, I thought, but I didn't say it. I'd been in enough trouble for the evening.

"You staying for Big Brother, little brother?" I asked him. That was the high-point of our mother-daughter-grandcat night, three episodes of Big Brother. Remember to pray to the Patron Saint of DVR's. Another joke I couldn't make while Mom was in a pretend-huff, but she would laugh later.

"Nope, got people to do, stuff to see," Manny said. "Unless you have more great school stories, or pictures of Nipplegate."

"That was Janet Jackson, this was The Nipple Riot, and I don't have any photos, The Whale stole my camera."

"Was this Orville's going away party?" Mom asked.

"Yeah, but it wasn't much of a party. Both the cake and the pizza ended up on the floor in the atrium, and Mr. H. and his replacement had to clean up the mess while I was restraining Munch for 45 minutes."

"Sounds like quite a send-off," Manny said, kissing Mama on the cheek as she opened another beer. He mischievously rattled Edna's bag as he went by, but she was not a cat to dart out startled, ever. She sauntered out, and began licking her paw and wiping it roughly across her eyes, the kitty sign language for get lost. And he did, finally.

"See ya', sis," he said, slamming the door, and then he was roaring his Camaro to life.

I picked up Edna and joined mom in the living room. Edna stretched out between us on the couch. She was long enough to rest her head in my lap and flick her tail into mom's ashtray.

I was glad that Edna liked to join me in the bubble bath; otherwise, she'd smell like a bar all weekend.

"You should be nicer to your brother, Ellie," Mom said. I turned on the TV and fast forwarded through the scenes from last week and the initial commercials. Mom dug her fingers into Edna's belly.

The cat purred and stretched. "He's the only family you got," she said.

"Edna's a girl," I said to her, but I knew she meant Manny.

"I won't live forever," Mom said, "and neither will this cat." She took a long swallow of beer, and exhaled smoke onto my cat. Nope, they could not live forever.

"Don't you think that having a grandbaby would be nice, Mama? Then we'd have some more family."

"I do have a grandbaby," Mom said, stroking Edna's fat raccoon tail. "My little Eddie."

"No, really. If Manny's going to be screwing around—and you know he does—it would be nice to have a little Manny," I couldn't believe I was saying those words.

I used to say I loved kids and that's why I fell into education. The truth was I hated kids, and I was eager to turn them into literate, productive, tax-paying adults. When I got assigned to the Narcissistic Praise-Junkies unit, I decided to give up on that, and go for teaching future prison inmates to read enough to write letters to their Lonely Hearts Club sweethearts and know how many cigarettes one should get for blowing a guard versus a high-rung, well-hung inmate.

"And with a little Manny comes a little wifey," Mom said, sipping her beer. "Babies need to be raised in families. You know how you suffered without a father. And yes, having a baby would be nice, but spouses are too much trouble. They change you. It's not another half makes a whole, like they say, but a whole lot of have-to that makes you half what you were. Or could be."

"That makes no sense, Mama."

"You have a family, Ellie."

"I know. You, Manny and Edna are the only family I'll ever have. I'm 32, my time to be tempted to the dark side is past, but Manny's just 26. We could find him a nice Catholic girl."

"Then they'd have ten kids, and we'd never see him or the kids, because they'd be over at her parents' house with the little grandkids' fifty-six cousins."

"That is quite a fantasy, Mom," I scoffed.

"I'll tell you what a fantasy is, sissy, a fantasy is a happy-ever-after family life. You know what the word wife originally meant? Proto-Indo-European. 'Weip' is to twist, turn or wrap. As in twist us to another's will. Or 'ghwibh' meaning shame. Possibly the Dutch 'wiif' or bitch, and that's what being a wife turns you into." Mama loved words as much as I did. No wonder I'd become an English teacher.

"That's not true, it just means woman," I argued.

"But 'husband' that means caretaker," she continued, ignoring me. "And how many husbands are that, huh?" Mom raised her voice and Edna jumped down and I heard her creep onto the porch.

Mom lit a cigarette, took a drag, and continued more calmly, "Women do the caretaking, bear the shame, and turn bitter. If Manny got married he'd turn into a selfish slug of a man—"

"Just like his father," I finished.

"No, like every man. And it turns us mean."

With this, I remembered why Mom was not allowed beer. We would also have to prohibit bake sales, obviously.

After our own exciting conflict, reality television seemed a little slow. Mom must have thought so too; she dozed off at the beginning of the second episode. I collected the beer cans and loaded the dishwasher, then took one of Mama's cigarettes and went to sit on the porch with Edna.

When I reached to heft her onto my shoulders, she growled and swatted at me. "I know, you don't like it, but if you can tolerate it from your grandmother, it won't hurt you if I have a cigarette once in a while."

I petted her head and scratched her ear, and she gave in and rolled over, freeing the cicada that she'd been sitting on. A little kitty vibrator. "Maybe that's what I need instead of this," I took a drag off the cigarette. That's what

Manny has, in those random girls. And what Daddy had, for a while. Maybe that's what I should get Mom for her birthday. A vibrator, not a cicada.

There is a smell to the school that I did not notice when I attended the high school for four years. And I don't think I noticed it during my seven years in general education. It's the smell that indicates they've washed down the floors with the same dirty mop-water they've been using for weeks or years, and the generic Pine-Sol—mixed with splashed urine, teenage zit ooze, seeds and stems, and general dirt and detritus—has gone rancid. When I was an English teacher, and when I was a student, the school smelled like sharpened pencils, new Crayons, and clean notebook paper. It had smelled like potential.

The NP students had been some of my favorite students when I was in the regular classroom just teaching English. They had stories to tell. They loved the free-writing time, a time for them to tell me—someone who would finally listen, I told myself—how they were left behind, misunderstood.

When Coach White took over as principal, he decided that there needed to be a "real teacher" in the specialty units. He'd had a grudge against me since I'd beaten him in the science fair our seventh grade year so he moved me into behavior. And the only non-coaching history teacher got put into the life skills unit. It was easier to find an English teacher than a behavior teacher, and having an opening in the history department was like inventing a new sport. I think Ms. Williams' replacement coached golf or bowling or water polo.

"These are dangerous, self-centered manipulative little punks," Mr. Humphrey said on my first day, after I'd given him my sunshine song and dance about their possibilities. I was actually pleased with the re-assignment, I'd told him, especially since I still got to teach English.

"How long you been in education?" the black man asked from behind his handkerchief. He filled it full of phlegm and returned it to his pocket.

"Well, I'm no teenager, you know," I said, but he apparently was not a fan of *The Miracle Worker*. Mr. Humphrey didn't know me, though, I reasoned. I had never called the unit asking him to come get one of his kids. I didn't write referrals to the office and fight over determination hearings. I knew how to handle these kids and I had a college degree, which made me automatically qualified.

But it turned out that he was right. Before the semester was over, I had christened the kids the Narcissistic Praise-Junkies as a group, and chosen the codenames: "Hangster the Gangster" for my suicidal African-American, "Genghis" for the arsonist with Down syndrome. The crack baby, at fourteen, was "Shattered" and "Aryan" was my young skinhead.

I had to remember their names, of course, for when I addressed them or talked to their parents. But their being anonymous, reduced to their behaviors or disorders, was easier when—at the end of the year—one was dead, two were in juvie, and one was a missing runaway. They were like dodgy acquaintances; with concentration I could match the name with the face, then with the outcome.

The new kid would just have to be "Brian" for a while. Unfortunately, he wasn't very bright, so he couldn't be "Brain," at least not right away—unless we were able to quickly determine that the name held the quota of irony required. He'd been in our school for a couple of weeks, and he claimed he was a junior, having been homeschooled for the past ten years, although there was no transcript to review.

His mom agreed to the unit because she saw it as a smaller, more supportive environment. She had no idea what she was exposing her boy to. He'd had several referrals for being disruptive, and I thought that what he would really need was just some social skills instruction. He needed to learn how to be in school. I could do that.

"Listen up, ladies and gentlemen," I said. My voice sounded forced, almost mechanical, even to me. Having a new student and a new adult in the room made me self-conscious. This was a lesson I had taught for a while, though. Even when I was a teacher in general education, I at least addressed the topic. Identify your feelings. You need to do it when you read and when you write, and any time you had to deal with any other human on the planet.

"How did you guys feel on Friday?" I turned to Brian and explained. "We had planned a party on Friday, but we had some behavior that caused us to have to cancel. I think it was kind of scary and disappointing. So I was frightened and

45

sad." I looked at my class. All of my kiddos had to attend class each day to learn social skills. Or "how to be with others without killing or being killed."

"I was pissed," Booger said, glaring at Munch's shoes.

"Nathan was angry. Right, Nathan? Angry?" I introduced Booger to Brian and corrected his word choice.

"Yeah, I was angry," he confirmed, now looking at my neck.

"Can I get some eye contact on that?" Nathan raised his eyes just a fraction, maybe to my nose, and repeated his confirmation.

"I thought it was hilarious," Trampy said, dancing the edge of her t-shirt up just a little.

"That's not a feeling, Jacky," I said. "Do you need help?"

"No. I was amused," she said.

"Hm. I wonder what was behind your behavior. You jumped into a bad situation and made it worse instead of better."

"I was just bored."

"I'm not sure about that. I think it was a really good day. A going-away party, pizza and cake for lunch. A new teacher. Sounds very unboring to me," I said.

"I just wanted the attention, I think," she said. I wondered if she was saying that because it was her guess at what I wanted to hear.

"Okay, so a little left out?"

"Did you think you needed to impress me?" Krista asked.

"I don't even know you," Jacky dismissed her.

"Maybe some anxiety too. Most people have more than one feeling at a time," I said, which was really my main message for this lesson. "Okay, y'all, who else has some feelings?"

"I'm really sorry," Munch said to his belly, which was all he could talk to since he was hunched almost in two. He was a pretty tall kid, and he was always hunched over, his shoulder length greasy hair curtaining his face.

"Who are you talking to?" I asked him.

"You," he said, looking at me. I raised my eyebrows. He corrected himself, "Everybody. Nathan. Everybody," he mumbled. He refused to open his mouth very wide since he'd had his front tooth knocked out while he was receiving his "brain injury," described in the records as a trampoline accident.

"So you just have the one feeling, remorse?" I asked.

He coughed out his tears, raising his hands to cover his face. "No, I guess, shame. I'm ashamed of myself," but I

47

could hear the lightness, almost laughter, in his voice. But he was a good liar.

"Shame is a hard feeling to have," I said. The Count, Becca, patted his shoulder. "When we are full of emotions, maybe to the point of not being able to contain them, I say we are full. A five," I held up my hand with my fingers extended. "We feel that our emotions are shooting in all directions." I traced an arc out of each of my fingertips. "So you cry or rage. It's maybe a little overwhelming." Munch nodded his head and Brian rolled his eyes.

"Brian, are you having any feelings about your change in schedule? You've only been here a very short time. How are you feeling about so much going on?" I nodded toward my hand, and raised my fingers one at a time.

"I don't know," he shrugged.

"Well, I hope you can think about it and let us know." I moved on to Krista. We had the conversation we'd planned over our carob chip oatmeal this morning, before we'd practiced choke holds and restraints on each other. She'd been a fierce opponent, and I felt silly for worrying about leaving her alone, unprotected, with the children.

When I'd asked her how she stayed so fit, she'd told me, "My boyfriend beats me. Or tries to." He was in prison now, she'd explained. I wondered if it was just for beating his girlfriend.

To the kids she said, "I was really nervous when I got here, but after the episode in the hall, I think I was really scared. I didn't feel good about coming to work today," she said. We hadn't rehearsed that last part, but it was perfect.

"Thanks, Ms. Parker, that was honest and very brave," I said. "I love that you guys shared your feelings today. Now, let's all check out our shoelaces, and let everyone have some privacy while they share their feeling-ratings with me." The students and Krista raised their fingers to me. Everyone extended all five fingers except for Twitch, Trevor. Having Tourette's syndrome, he always functioned at a five; he extended only his one middle finger. It would be a tough day on the unit, as usual.

Once all the other NP's had gone to class, I sat down with Brian to review his schedule. "Hey, you have any idea why your schedule got changed?" I asked him to start.

"My mom wanted me in a smaller class," he answered.

"Well that worked, huh? Now you're one of eight. Does that feel better?"

"I don't know. I've always been one of one," he shrugged.

"Okay, but the regular classroom was a little much?"

"No, it was fine. Just Mr. Principal-Dude called me in and gave me the new schedule. Said he'd talked to Mom."

"Hmm, it didn't seem totally fine. Sounded like you'd had some trouble?" But he didn't respond. "Not all your classes have changed. Still, Ms. Parker will walk you down to your same American history class. She's going to stay right outside the door, okay? So if you get anxious during class, you can just look right out the window and see her," I said nodding to the rectangular window in my own door. "Coach Windsor knows that if you need to walk out, you are going to head straight out the door, without disrupting the class, and Ms. P. will bring you right back here. Okay?"

"Yeah," he said.

"Y'all better get going or you'll have just as much nerves walking in late, right?"

"Yeah," he said. I was glad that the Home School had provided such great vocabulary instruction.

I had Trixie, Booger, and Twitch settled in for English when Krista returned twenty minutes later from what should have been a fifty minute vigil in the history wing. Her shirt, pale pink with a fake

Juicy Couture emblem, was now a sweat darkened patchwork with missing rhinestones. Her eye make-up smeared lines down her face and met on her chin like an Amish beard.

We had read the beginning of "Araby" and were discussing the author's purpose. "The author uses 'blind' in three different ways in just the first few paragraphs. What kind of tone does this set?" I didn't listen to their answers but to Krista's muffled sobbing. "How else does Joyce let you know about his or the characters' feelings?" Again, I didn't listen, but answered, "Yeah, right. Exactly." And followed up with, "If you were going to draw a picture of the unnamed narrator's neighborhood, what colors would you need? What colors would you avoid?"

Krista cried, tucked into the corner, until A-lunch began, and I handed out free lunch tickets, which the kids believed came from me but which really came from a government grant for at-risk kids. The feds started early in providing three squares—or at least two, breakfast and lunch—for their future inmates. No shank required.

When the bell rang, and the kids jumped from their chairs, I refrained from giving my normal, "The bell does not dismiss you. I dismiss you," and just let them go. Fishsticks, French fries, and Otis Spunkmeyer were hard to compete against, and I didn't have the motivation today. As soon as the door closed, I flung myself down on the couch next to Krista, but she turned away, into herself, like a rape victim.

"What happened?" I kept my voice casual. I was positive that it couldn't be worth all the body fluid she was shedding. She plunged her face into the pillows and snotted and heaved for several minutes before she quieted.

"He looked at me," she said.

"Oh my God, who? Who looked at you? Did he turn to stone?" I said.

She stopped crying. Scornful skeptic and horrified victim are two roles that one cannot play simultaneously, even at a five. She sighed heavily and gulped a breath. "I didn't know what he was doing, but it was something. He just kept looking at me, and when I reached for the door, he smiled and tipped his head back, like a nod. An invitation. And when I opened the door, I could hear his hand hitting his desk. The chair was squeaking," Krista was crying again. She looked at my blank face. "Rhythmically," she added gravely.

"And you left him there?" I screeched, jumping up, then sitting down again realizing he would be in chemistry by now.

"He wasn't finished," she said.

"That's why you should have brought him back."

"Gross. To finish?"

"Well, here there are just two adults to be exposed to it instead of a roomful of kids."

"Exposed," she faked a Munch giggle, but when her face scrunched up, I couldn't tell if it was the mime of a laugh or a cry.

"Let's deal with this before the kids get back from lunch," I said mostly to myself. I was frustrated as much by Krista as Brian. I picked up the phone to call the coach's lounge. It's like a teacher's lounge except there's a television, healthy snacks, and a functioning coffee maker, and it was more crowded because there were more sports to coach than subjects to teach. "Go wash your face," I told her gruffly.

"May I speak with Coach Windsor?" I asked the guy who answered the phone saying, cleverly, "This is Coach." I pictured a meaty hand covering the mouthpiece. I could hear the muffled snickers as the Coach made his way to the phone. Coach Meaty took his paw off the receiver a smidge too early, and I heard my own cruel nickname.

"Freakshow? Why didn't ya' tell her I wasn't here, Sam?" I heard the phone being transferred from hand to hand. "Hello."

"Hey, Coach. It's Ellie, The Freakshow. My I.A. said that Brian—"

"Your what?" he interrupted.

"My instructional assistant," I said. My irritation rose. "Krista. She told me that Brian was masturbating during class."

"What the heck? She says you were beating off during my class, Edwards," he said to the room.

"No, not Coach Brian," I said patiently, but not too patiently. "The new kid in my unit. Brian Stevens. So, yeah? He was?"

"How the hell should I know? I was reviewing game film. He'll have something to whack to next week, 'cause we are gonna' fuck the Indians Friday night." The lounge erupted in cheers and whoops. "The film will be like a porno."

I hung up. I hate the word porno. Why that extra syllable? Didn't just "porn" say it all?

"He was reviewing game film." I told Krista. "So the lights were out?"

"Yeah, I guess so. They were."

"Good, maybe not everybody saw it. As least I know the type of class disruption he caused to get here. You okay?"

"I'm good. Better. Sorry, I'm just shaken up."

"I know. It's okay. You haven't visited the prison much have you?" I asked, teasingly, but actually curious.

"No, not yet," she answered seriously. "I can't make myself go."

Krista had endured enough trauma for one day without relationship analysis. "Do you think our social skills lesson tomorrow should be about washing hands?"

"Keeping your hands to *yourself*," she lowered her voice to husky purr on the last word.

"Keeping private parts private?"

"When to have eye contact and when to avoid it."

"That's a good one, I might actually need to teach that," I said, writing it on a sticky note and putting it on the cover of my lesson plan book.

"You know, I'm going to have to call his mother. That's why he got put in here. The other teachers and the A.P. couldn't tell her what he was doing."

"Crybabies," she said, opening the snack cabinet. "What's for lunch?"

―――――――

I kept Brian in the room for the rest of the day and had Krista pick up his work from his out-classes. During English, I told him pointedly that I needed to see his hands at all times. The Whale laughed but not too loudly. He didn't want to take on Brian until he'd had enough time to evaluate his weaknesses.

I called Brian's mom as soon as he left for the carpool line. I wanted to be able to reach her before he got in the car, but I needed to hear how she approached him with it. Would she be a crier, or a yeller, or a hitter? It was important for me to learn that now so I could know when and how to make phone calls in the future.

"Mrs. Stevens?" I asked when she picked up the phone. "This is Ellie Warden from Brian's school. I wanted to tell you how his first day was with his new schedule."

"Thank you. That is so sweet. That's just why I wanted him switched, he was getting lost in the crowd. I haven't heard from one of his teachers since he's been there," she said, confirming what I'd thought about my cowardly colleagues. She rattled on, "And I've had him at home with me all of his life until I had to start working." I heard her voice break. "When my husband and I separated." Having her cry now would skew my results, so I plunged in.

"Since you haven't talked to Brian's teachers, I'm assuming no one has told you that your son has been masturbating in class?"

"What? No. Oh my God."

"There have been several referrals for disruption, and when I talked to the referring teachers today, they described the nature of the disruption. And my co-teacher saw him today in history class. Masturbating."

I felt her steel herself after her initial breakdown. She took a deep breath. "He's had a really hard time adjusting to school. There are so many things that I never thought to tell him."

"Like not to masturbate during instruction? Did he do that when you were homeschooling him?"

"Well, he was mostly by himself during that time, you know, watching the History Channel or National Geographic. So I'm sure that he did some multi-tasking."

"Multi-tasking," I said back, just so Krista could get a sense of the conversation. I heard the car door open and Brian's voice through the phone.

"I'm on the phone. Just a minute, sweetie," she said to him. "Well, thanks for letting me know," she said breezily to me.

"You're welcome. And thanks for talking to him tonight to let him know that his behavior is not only disruptive but could be considered criminal. I'm sure he'll be much more comfortable having that conversation with you than with me," I said and hung up.

"Are you kidding me?" Krista asked.

"Nope, another home-school victim. Mom never told him that you eat your meat, not beat your meat. It's not his fault." For all the behavior I saw from the kids in the NP unit, they were shockingly not responsible for most of it. "Do you think we should call him 'Vic' for home-school victim? Or maybe, Brian the Beater?" I asked Krista.

The phone rang, two short rings to indicate an internal call. Thank God, I was not ready to confront another mother today. "Ellie, it's Coach Sanders. I need you to come get Nathan."

Crap, crap, crap, I thought. I hated these jocks, I missed the days they'd just shove me in a locker or fake-invite me to prom, but whining all the time was pissing me off. "I'm off duty, Coach. I don't get paid for afterhours care," I told him.

"You get him, or the police get him because I can't reach any of the assistant principals." The A.P.'s were responsible for discipline.

"Dammit," I said, gathering up my belongings. "What's he done?"

"He spray-painted graffiti on the wall of my field house."

"Oh no," I groaned. That was serious. "You sure it was Nathan?"

"No doubt, he got as much paint on himself as he did on my wall."

"Okay, I'll call his mom on my way," I said, and I grabbed my iPhone and hurried out, leaving Krista, clueless, behind me.

The room where we had our special education meetings was more like a closet. It was windowless with minimal table space—to keep parents and advocates from bringing too much documentation paperwork—and we all sat up on top of each other. It was the same concept as keeping it ridiculously cold in a restaurant; you don't want people to hang around longer than they need to.

The tension of the meeting was always directly proportional to the number of people in attendance. Booger's Manifestation Determination hearing was packed. Coach Sanders sat with Ms. Hale, Booger's algebra teacher, on one side of the table. I took a chair beside Booger and Booger's mom, Paula Harmon. The special education director and the school psychologist were seated at either end of the conference table. There was a chair available on either side of the table, and I wondered if anyone else was anticipating where the principal would sit when he arrived. This should not feel like a faceoff, but it did; Sanders wouldn't look in my face, though. I'd left a message playing the recording of his calling Trixie a fairy on his voicemail.

Our principal, Mr. White, had been Coach White on this campus before he was in administration, and he had played ball with Sanders in high school. That didn't necessarily mean that he would be biased, but I did not trust him. The ARD meeting did not have to be unanimous, but if there were more than a couple of dissenters, it would get complicated.

A hearing like this would be called when a student who receives special education services was facing disciplinary action. It would be up to the committee, those of us at the table plus the principal, to decide whether or not the student's behavior was due to his disability.

Because of his Asperger's syndrome, Booger may or may not face suspension due to his painting on the field house. We would decide as a committee. If we decided against suspension, we would have to agree on what consequences he would face.

Mr. White walked into our awkward silence at precisely 2:00. He took a chair beside Coach Sanders.

"Howdy, Coach," he said, plopping down, then he stood up part way and held his hand out to Paula Harmon, "Ma'am." It's like the rest of us weren't even there. He acknowledged only his buddy and his constituent obligation. "Let's get this show on the road."

The school psychologist, Chelsea, a youngster of twenty-four years old, opened her green folder. It was about 4 inches thick, indicating a child who had been in special education his entire academic career. "The purpose of this meeting today is to determine what, if any, disciplinary action should be taken against Nathan Harmon for defacing and vandalizing school property. The administration has suggested a three day suspension. The parent, Dr. Paula Harmon, has objected to this action. All parties will abide by the decision of the majority vote of this committee."

Chelsea handed out copies and then read aloud from the referral form, which reported that on the afternoon of August 22, between school dismissal at 3:45 and the commencement of football practice at 4:15, Nathan took a can of black spray paint from a locker in the boys' dressing room and wrote, "Coach

Sanders is a doush-bag," in letters approximately four to six inches high on the outside of the field house.

"That behavior does not sound like my son," Paula jumped in as soon as the description of the incident was finished.

"Who wrote this?" I asked, indicating the referral form. I recognized Nathan's handwriting.

"What difference does it make?" Coach asked, with no trace of satisfaction in his voice.

"Nathan wrote it," I said quietly. Not sure what this would mean for my kid.

"Why?" Chelsea asked Coach Sanders.

"It don't matter who wrote it, does it? We're not disagreeing over whether or not he did it, and why should we? He told us right here what happened." Sanders said. "There's no reason to argue over guilt or innocence."

Dr. Harmon bristled. "We most assuredly are discussing his culpability. For some reason my son adores you so he would never write such a thing. Secondly, he would never use the word douche bag, and if he did he would have spelled it correctly. He spells everything correctly."

"Come on," Coach said, "when he went to spray the wall, he had the nozzle turned around and he sprayed himself right in the face, he looked like a Hell's Angel. And he wrote his confession," he pointed his finger at the referral. Finally the satisfaction.

"Dr. Harmon is right. This doesn't sound like Nathan's typical behavior," I said. "Perhaps the idea wasn't his? Could he have been put up to this? Children with Asperger's syndrome are very susceptible to suggestion."

"Children?" Paula scoffed. "Anyone with Asperger's. My brother, who's thirty-five, does everything he's told. We own a veterinary practice together, and he does all the impacted anal glands that come in. Why? Because he's told to."

"So he's a thirty-two year old doctor who does whatever he's told to do?" I asked. "Is he married?" After Paula laughed, everyone joined in, not sure at first if my joke was okay. Everyone at the table, except the parent, was accustomed to my jokes not being entirely appropriate.

"No, he is not. But that's just the point. A man, and even more so a boy, with an autistic spectrum disorder cannot be responsible for himself. Peter could never be married, maintain any sort of relationship outside of the one he has with me and Nathan. We understand his disability. I know, for example, that if I tell my brother to 'go jump in a lake,' I'll have to identify his bloated body a week later when it washes up on the banks of Lady Bird Lake.

"Like his uncle Peter, Nathan is very smart. But he's not creative and he's not destructive. If he did this," she stopped herself. "Since he did this thing, we have to assume that someone put him up to it."

"Did you ask him who?" Mr. White probed skeptically.

"Of course. But someone told him not to tell. And an Aspy is faithful to his word. He will never tell."

Of course I'd worked with students with Asperger's before, but I'd never considered that there may be good qualities. Nathan was a fourteen year-old mouth-breathing, booger-eating, spit-bubble blowing, shamelessly farting, preachy smarty-pants. But his mom obviously saw the B side; he was also loyal, faithful, honest, and obliging. Like a good Labrador retriever.

At the beginning of the semester, when the coach had met Nathan, who had signed up for boys' athletics to be a trainer—which basically meant water-boy when one was a freshman—he had stormed the unit like a swarm of Africanized bees.

"He drools in the Gatorade, picks his nose while he's handing out clean towels, stares at the men in the shower, and corrects my play-calling." I'd attended practice the next day instead of the less exciting but more air-conditioned teacher training that marks the beginning of the new school year.

The boys were doing two-a-day practices. When I'd arrived, Nathan was explaining to a group of linemen the biological reason and significant benefits of sweating. They looked ready to kill him, but that was nothing compared to the coach. When he'd called his boys to huddle up, Nathan had scolded him not to interrupt.

"I cannot have that boy with my kids," he'd blared.

"He is one of your kids now," I'd answered hotly.

"No. No, no, no. This is your kid. Your kind of kid. I have athletes."

"You have students. This is your student."

"Not for long." And I guess Coach was right. It was only Wednesday of the third week of school. It maybe wouldn't be long.

"So we are looking at three days of suspension," I turned the conversation to what had to be the ultimate conclusion. "What lesson should Nathan learn from that?" I asked the men. "And what lesson *will* he learn from that?" I asked Paula.

"He will learn to respect school property and personnel," Coach Sanders said loudly, slamming his fist on the table.

"Since we are not your athletes, we do not have helmets obstructing our hearing so there is no reason to yell," I said.

"What's your recommendation, Ellie?" Chelsea asked stopping me before I started a war.

"Three days in ISS."

"Fine," Coach nodded, "in school suspension will still prevent him from—"

"And he works the opening game on Friday night," I said, cutting him off. I saw that this was really the goal: get Nathan off the sidelines for the game. Once a trainer missed a game, he was practice trainer only. Coach *was* a douche bag.

"That's against school policy," Mr. White said abruptly.

"So is failing to investigate possible bullying. And conspiracy. And, I'm sure, letting one disabled student take the fall for what an entire club had a hand in. Nathan said he got the paint from a locker. Does he even have a locker? I wouldn't think so. Don't all of the lockers have locks? Isn't that school policy?"

"ISS until noon on Friday then? Getting out at noon will allow him to attend the game," Chelsea concluded, already passing around the signature sheet.

I walked Paula to her car, which is what I always do after special education meetings. I like for the committee to see me on the parent's side. I especially like for the parent to see me on the parent's side, which keeps them from harassing me for the most part. If they harass me as a habit, I follow them to the parking lot in case I have to identify their car. Either because it ran me off the road or because I need to provide some design modification later. Or at least fantasize about it.

When we got through the atrium and out the door, Paula started to sniff. By the time we were at her Cadillac Escalade, there were slight but determined tears coming from her eyes.

"Thank you for understanding how important the game is to Nathan," she said robotically and stuck out her hand.

"You can thank me by introducing me to your doctor brother who does what he's told and always stays faithful to his word."

She laughed, and relaxed a little, leaned against her car. "No, I actually like you. I wouldn't want you to have to deal with my son all day and then my brother too."

This time I offered my hand, and she hugged me. But I'm pretty sure she wiped her nose on my shoulder at the same time. "We'll see you at the game," Paula said, happy again, and left.

6

The phone trilled its single long out-of-the-building ring. Somebody's mother. There were generally two kinds of parents of special education students: those who were really into their kids (over-parenting), and those who were really into their kids' disabilities (under-parenting).

With the latter, you were likely to hear the kid's primary, secondary, and tertiary qualifying condition before you heard his or her name. And some of them used their children's disorder as their own: I'm an autism mom, or a Down syndrome parent. A badge of honor; a look-at-me, I'm a long-suffering parent, a praise-junkie. It was like PFLAG for the physically, emotionally or mentally handicapped rather than the lesbian or gay child.

Naturally, there were parents who didn't give a damn about their kids or their kids' conditions. They didn't call my room. They were busy.

"New Pathways, this is Ellie Warden," I said into the receiver. We were now at a point where I could take the phone, or take a pee, and Krista would pick up right where I left off. She had a range of activities that kept the kids engaged if I had to leave in the middle of a lesson.

"Ellie?" Mom asked.

"Hey, Mom, what's going on?" She didn't normally call me during the school day unless there was an emergency. Of course, Mom's definition of emergency and an actual emergency are two separate things.

"Oh, Ellie," she cried, "I'm just sick. I'm not going to be able to go to the game with y'all tonight."

"Oh no, Mom, why?" Mom and I, and usually Manny, went to every home football game. I had played the flute in my high school marching band, and Manny had been a running back for the varsity team starting in his sophomore year. It was a long tradition.

"I'm sick. I just told you."

"I thought you were sick about not being able to go," I said.

"I am. Who's on first," Mom laughed, but it turned into a groan. Mom loved to play with words even when she was sick.

"I've got the runnin' off and pukes. It's about to run me to death."

Trixie erupted in a fit of giggles. The kids were taking turns showing off their best touchdown dances. Twitch spiked an imaginary football and raised his hands to the sky, "Thank you, Jesus!" he exclaimed. It turned into a tic. "Jesus, flapping, mother-flapper, Jesus! Jesus!" He slapped the back of his hand into his face. Poor thing. He hated losing control. No one was laughing now. Even among my kids, they saw Twitch's disorder as truly sad and crippling. The rest of them talked about their bad decisions or inappropriate choices. Twitch's compulsion just highlighted the others' ability to choose.

"What in the badlands is that?" Mom asked. "These kids today, they'll say anything. Do you let them talk like that in your classroom?"

I didn't want Twitch to overhear my describing his disorder to a stranger, but Brian, the new kid, seemed as distraught as Mom. Whacking off while leering at your teacher was apparently normal to him. Cursing the Savior was not.

"Mom," I said loudly and paused. I wanted Twitch to know that I wasn't talking to another parent or the air conditioning repair man. "Trevor has Tourette's syndrome, which is a neurological disorder. His brain insists that he do things such as jerk his neck, blink his eyes repeatedly, or make certain sounds or words. Trevor has a few tics, vocalization of obscenities, stretching out his neck, putting his hand to his face." I was hoping that I could suggest to Trevor's brain that he didn't need to slap himself to fulfill the brain's compulsion, but my words got swallowed up when the final bell rang, and the kids stampeded out the door with Krista following behind like she was herding cats. I dropped into my chair. It had been quite a week. Friday felt good.

"Well, I hope to Goodness that they neuter that child," Mom said.

"Neutering is a form of birth control, you know." I knew she'd only been teasing, but Mom's inconsistencies about the doctrine and catechism frustrated me. She had always insisted I learn it, love it, and live it, but she could say anything.

"Yeah, well, find out if his family is Catholic. There's nothing wrong with neutering the Protestants, right?" she laughed weakly. "And if he is Catholic, they should get him exorcised," she said.

"Yep, I guess either way there's some way to take the devil out of him," I said. I didn't even introduce the idea that there might be other options besides

Catholic and Protestant. She wasn't up to that kind of debate. "What made you so sick, do you think?" I was thinking of some of the crappy food she'd secretly consumed, maybe something Manny provided, spoiled canned meat or something.

"Oh, it's just a bug. Some of the ladies at the Rosary club had it."

"You need to stop drinking after them at the sacramental cup. Elbow your way to the front next time."

"You could block for me." Mama and I attended mass every week day morning at 6:00, but she let me sleep in on Saturday; confession didn't start until 10:00

"Sorry you're going to miss the first game, Mama." And I was.

"Me too, honey, but it won't be long before we have the Longhorns on Saturday and the Cowboys on Sunday," she tried to sound cheerful.

Krista came back in just as I was hanging up. "Anything wrong?" she asked.

"No, Mom just can't go to the game tonight. We always go together."

"That sounds fun. I wish I was close with my mom," she said.

"Where's your mom?"

"Gatesville," she said.

"That's not so far. You could still see her every couple of weeks."

"Yeah, I do. But visitation is short and doesn't give enough time to really bond. And no football games, the Texas penal system frowns on field trips."

I was embarrassed. Gatesville was the women's maximum security prison. I wondered what her life must be like. Her mom and her boyfriend in prison. I didn't want to ask about her father.

I used Munch's guttural snicker, ala Beevis and Butthead, "You said 'penal.'"

"God, Ellie, you're as bad as the kids."

"That's why they keep me here," I answered, pulling out our behavior log to document the fun times we'd had that day. "You want to go to the game with me? My brother probably won't go if Mom doesn't."

"Your family's like a little cult," she laughed, pulling out her notebook of the days deeds and misdeeds. "Why aren't you married?" Krista asked bluntly.

"Don't hold back, sweetie, you need to ask your questions, use your words, feel your feelings," I said, hoping to deflect by quoting the phrases we said to the kids hundreds of times a day.

"Sorry, we talk about so much personal stuff with the kids," Krista turned red. "Including boundaries. We talk about those with the kids." Krista recorded The Whale's holding down Trixie so Munch could fart in her face. Boundaries.

"No, it's okay. That's a normal question to ask. I'm hot, funny, brilliant, successful, and compassionate. I should have been married two or three times by my age."

"How old are you?"

"Wow, you are on a mission to break through all those boundaries today, huh? I'm 32, and I've never been married because that is how my mama raised me." Krista looked quizzical, and I could see her stifling her questions.

I logged on the parent contact form Munch's mom's request that we clean the desks, doorknobs, and stapler with Lysol. I'd hate to make her son sick. "We're Catholic, and my parents had a rotten marriage, according to my mom. My dad died when I was six. Mama was pregnant with my brother at the time. The worst part is that my mom and dad really loved each other. I believe that. And I believe that I remember that. Mom even says it, but she also says that marriage ruined it.

"When I was a teenager, and determined to find a husband—or at least a boyfriend—she would say, 'At least be smart enough to go for money.' And 'There's nothing like being in love to ruin falling in love.' I never fell for a guy with money so I never got married."

"Wow. Did you ever fall for a guy at all?" Krista asked.

"Not enough to risk both the disapproval of my mother and the supposed unavoidable destruction of whatever feeling was present. Think about it. No possibility of divorce for any reason, coupled with the utter certainty that marriage will kill the love. And, I feared, the love of my family. It wasn't worth it."

"What about now? Surely you've realized by now that your parents' marriage is not the prototype for all marriages everywhere eternally," Krista said, flipping the pages in her spiral.

"If only to have children, I would get married. But I couldn't deal with the disappointment of losing someone I loved. Or losing the love and having to keep the someone. That would be worse." I thought for a second.

"Say I was to find a nice Catholic man who made plenty of money and wanted to sweep me off my feet and take care of my every need and whim forever with nothing in return except very occasional access to my baby-making parts? That might work, as long as I didn't love him. See, the love makes the marriage too risky. Or so I've believed for so long now it's hard to change my mind."

"So you'll get married as soon as you find someone you hate?"

"Hates not necessary. Just ambivalence. Like maybe he was mute and blind. Or he had boils all over his body so he couldn't accept excessive touching like cuddling and stuff."

"Great. So if a leper and Helen Keller's ghost have a baby, you'll be on him like flies on road kill."

"Yep. That's my plan. Until then, I have my cat. Oh, my unclean deaf-mute has to be Catholic and like my cat. And want children." I thought for a minute, as long as I was creating the perfect husband-material, I should do it right. "And be wealthy. Maybe a workaholic so he isn't around much."

"You should get a prison boyfriend who's allowed conjugal visits. A mobster with a secret stash of money."

"Perfect," I said. "You got an Incident Report?"

"Yeah, I started it." Krista handed it to me.

The Whale. Krista had had to pull down his binder to find his real name: Walter. She'd recorded the initials of the children and the names of the adults present. "You didn't put Officer Hotty on here?"

"No, he was only here for the aftermath. Plus, I don't know his name. It's not Hotty, is it?"

"It's on his name tag. Webber." I added it to the witnesses.

"Sorry, Ellie, when he's around, I'm not looking at his name tag."

Krista tidied up and watered the plants while I wrote the gory details. The Whale's computer science teacher had called the room for an escort, and Krista had brought him back to the room where I was conducting English class with Munch and Becca. They were formatting friendly letters, writing from the "Araby" narrator to Mangan's sister or from the sister to the narrator.

Still ramped up from his outburst in the computer lab, The Whale walked in and immediately snatched Becca's letter off her desk and read it aloud. "I see you looking at me when I leave for school, and I walk more slowly when I hear your footsteps. I count them, and wait to see you. I've wanted to talk to you for I love you too."

When Becca tried to grab her letter out of his hands, he took the opportunity to cup his hand around her left breast, which was a double torture—having him touch her but only touching one side of her. She would be out of proportion all day.

Knowing he would be restrained if he continued the assault, he threw his hands up, like a basketball player proclaiming his innocence of the foul he'd just blatantly committed. "Your demerits will prohibit you from having lunch in the cafeteria today. You'll eat here with us," I told him calmly, letting Becca burrow her head into my armpit.

"Fuck that. Look like I'm used to missing my meals, bitch?" he said as he walked out the door.

I gave Krista the trembling girl, grabbed my keys and walkie, and followed The Whale into the hall. As he started down the stairs, I used my master key to disable the magnetic doorstops, so he was trapped in the stairwell. I grabbed the door as it swung shut and entered the stairwell with him. "Sweetie, you know I can't let you wander around the school when you're having such a hard time managing your emotions," I said walking down to the landing.

When he saw me, he started pounding on the door and shouting to be let out. Anyone watching would have thought the child was scared of me, although he was twice my weight and at least my height. I sat down on the top stair of the lower flight, trying to be non-threatening. Coach Davis, who ran in-school-suspension, ISS, knocked on the door, "You okay in there?"

"Yep. Situation normal," I said.

"Get me out of here," The Whale yelled, but the coach walked away. He was just a couple of doors down and was used to checking on me. I used the stairwell as my counseling room fairly often. Like Fonzie's bathroom. Step into my office.

The Whale turned his back on the door and slid down until he was sitting on his haunches. It occurred to me then that most gargoyles are skinny. I wondered why. I'd have to look that up. While I was ruminating on it, though, The Whale had dropped his pants. Most gargoyles also did not have pants, I thought, and was only brought to complete attention when I smelled it. Then it was too late; there was a large turd on the floor, and one in his hand. As he wound up to pitch it at me, I ducked and covered, but I felt the warm feces hit my upper arm and shoulder.

I stood and walked calmly up the stairs, The Whale, somewhat immobilized by his awkwardly balanced position over his growing pile, stayed behind. I unlocked the door and stepped into the hallway. "E.W. to S.R.O.," I said into the walkie.

"School Resource Officer Webber," the walkie answered.

"I've been assaulted by the student in stairwell A. The assault was serious and willful, and I will be pressing charges."

"I'll get him," he said.

"Can you call maintenance too? I'm not near my phone."

"You need medical?" he sounded concerned.

"Nope. Just a shower."

I had a locker in the girls' locker room. I was back in the classroom with fresh clothes and wet hair in time to watch from the window as The Whale was loaded into the police car.

"You wanna' proofread it for me, Krista?" I offered her the Incident Report.

"No, not really, but I am eager to read all the gory details," she said, taking it.

"Next time we have a student trapped in the stairwell, you're going in," I told her.

7

Football games should be cold, but in Texas the football season starts when it is still possible to die of a heat stroke during an evening game. Not just the players, either, any of us. The concession stand's biggest seller? Sno-cones. In central Texas, we can often wear shorts and t-shirts to every game of the season.

The trainers had to pay for both their short sleeved golf shirts with our emblematic savage on the left breast, and the sweatshirts that are rarely worn, but are never recycled from year to year since they are sold by the Booster Club. Students provide their own khaki pants, and Booger looked as cute as a midget on roller skates in his little uniform, with rolls of athletic tape cuffing each of his arms, and a belt that could hold six water bottles.

My family migrated from year to year. I'd had a student on the cheerleading squad in my first year, a schizophrenic with religious delusions. She wore a skirt down to her mid-calf and when the other girls stood at rest, their tight fists on their hips, she stood with her arms outstretched like the crucified Christ. Last year, The Whale had played the tuba, and Mama, Manny, and I had sat dutifully deafened by the band, but The Whale had not been invited back since he'd concussed one of his band mates with the kid's rented French horn.

This year I sat directly behind the team bench so I could encourage Nathan. I doubtfully saved a seat for my brother. He wouldn't come, I knew, if he didn't have to drive Mom. He was a little like that awkward uncle in Napoleon Dynamite, but he was much younger. Really, though, you only have to be nineteen or so before your glory days are behind you, unless you go to college. Manny wasn't bright enough to even break into a college, but he could break through that line when he was sixteen.

When I brought Mom, she had her full set-up: stadium seat, paper pom-poms, and she insisted on doing the Savage Feathers, which was no longer politically correct, but it had been fine when she had graduated from this school. The Feathers was when you put your two fingers up, kind of like a Scout pledge and stuck them to the side of your head above and behind your ear, like feathers in a chief's headdress. Mom also liked to do the Tomahawk Chop, which she'd seen in a news video clip fifteen years before when the Atlanta Braves were in the World Series.

Mom was unaware that the era when you could claim both the moniker "Savages" and the effigy of the red-faced Indian was over. Or should have been.

Sitting near my students allowed me to socialize with their parents and convinced the parents that I was interested in their children. It was nice that they got to meet my mother, as politically incorrect as she may be, because she normally charmed and amused them, and it allowed them to see me as a real person.

Once, teachers had been appreciated and respected. Now, we are often vilified and blamed by parents, especially when their child has acted villainously and been blamed. I was an especially good target because I had almost total access to, if not control of, my juvenile delinquents all day, every day.

I had enough good sense to at least expect the attacks from any parent so I had the usual amount of apprehension when Paula Harmon came and sat down in Manny's spot. I could have objected but when she got there, seconds before kick-off, I'd already concluded that my brother would not be joining me.

She was dressed in scrubs that had a tessellation of multi-colored cartoon kitties. I wanted to wear clothes like that to work. Restraints would be much easier if I weren't restricted by even my casual jeans and t-shirts. I was willing to bet that restraining a cat, or even a rabid German shepherd, was not as physically taxing or as challenging as holding down a mentally ill teenage boy with encopresis.

"What did I miss?" she asked.

"Nothing yet. Well, Nathan taped up some bench-sitters. Just practice, I guess."

"He practiced on me and his Uncle Peter. And our clinic kitty, Scratch. He should be pretty good at it now."

"Scratch, I like that. My cat is named Edna, she's a Maine coon."

"You bought a pure-bred cat? Do you know how many shelter cats are euthanized every day in this city?"

"Yeah, I should have rescued one, but I was in college when I got her, I didn't understand," I lied. I knew that plenty of people got their panties in a wad about over-priced cats, but I had wanted a Maine coon.

"And your cat's still alive?" she asked.

"Ouch. I'm only 32," I said.

"Oh, I'm sorry, that's not what I meant. Fourteen years is a long life for a cat, but when young people get pets, they don't always last long. Neglect. Ignorance."

"She just turned thirteen. She's always been very healthy; I tried to get educated before I got her. Researching is how I found out about Maine coons. I read they were easy to get along with, and it was my first cat."

"Where do you get her treated?"

"North Austin Cat Center," I said, feeling like I was being tested. I needed to take control of this conversation, or we would have the total inverse of the relationship I needed us to have. "I wanted a specialist."

"Well, you didn't get one. Those doctors who run those cat or bird or small animal hospitals, and especially the emergency shops, those are just vets that didn't master all they needed to in medical school," she said, sniffing.

I was reminded of the first day of school when I was getting all the kids organized: binders neatly labeled, dividers inserted, contraband confiscated. Nathan had assessed everyone's school supplies and labeled them substandard. "The Trapper Keeper is a far superior zippered binder to Mead," he'd explained to The Whale. "Big Lots, though, or the Dollar Store or wherever you can afford to shop, probably doesn't have the T.K."

Twitch, trying to be the peacemaker said, "Hey, that was a South Park episode. Remember? Cartman and his alien Trapper Keeper? Dr. Who or someone lived in there."

We started the social skills right away. Nathan was a freshman, but I always track my incoming students through their middle-school years. I attended their special education meetings throughout their eighth grade years so I knew Nathan. I knew Aspies. All students with Asperger's syndrome seem self-centered, but Nathan's weirdness manifested even more than normal as arrogance.

"I wonder how The Whale feels about your saying your belongings are superior," I said.

"I wonder how he feels about your calling him The Whale," he retorted.

"Let's ask him," I said. It was the wrong thing to say. He told Nathan that his name was The Whale, and Nathan countered that no loving mother would name her child that. It couldn't be on his birth certificate. The Whale sat on him and then ripped his Trapper Keeper in half and challenged Nathan to rip his Mead. Nathan, of course, could not.

Now, his mother's vet practice was superior to my vet's back-alley substandard snake-oil outlet. "Yeah," I nodded my head, ostensibly agreeing with her assessment of Edna's doctor, "but he gives free horse tranquilizers to his favorite clients. The humans, I mean." She looked shocked until I laughed.

"I'm sorry," she said. "I didn't mean to insult your doctor. I'm sure if you've taken your cat there for twelve years, you're pretty confident in his abilities. It's Dr. Rimey over there, right?"

"Yeah. Edna loves him. I share the tranquilizers with her if she's a good girl."

"Ah, so this is why Nathan reports that Ms. Parker is the nice one and Ms. Warden is the devil. He doesn't get your humor."

"I don't play with the kids like that," I said. "Well, not all the kids. Not Nathan. None of the students on the spectrum."

"Do you have others?"

"Not this year, thank God," I answered without thinking.

"Yeah, two is more than enough for me," she agreed.

"Does your brother live with you?" I asked.

"No, not anymore, thank God," she laughed. "We built him a little house behind the clinic. He can live there independently, and it's really helped with emergency care and the boarding business.

"He has a housekeeper. Personal assistant, really, to make sure he keeps appointments, wears matching shoes, eats real food." She sighed. "I was sure he couldn't live on his own, but he insisted. He was right, I guess."

"That's good. Sounds like it worked out best for everyone," I said.

"Don't tell him I told you all that. Any of that," she said, and I wanted to object that I wasn't likely to meet him, but she pointed. I thought she was shushing me for kick-off. The boys were lined up, and the whistle blew. But she was pointing down the field.

Walking out of the end zone, as though there weren't a football game going on at all, waving his arms above his head like he was singing and dancing to Monster Mash in his head, was Peter. Above the noise of the frantically whistling officials, the groaning coaches and players, and booing and cursing fans, you could hear him. "Nathan! Nathan! Look, I made it. Uncle Peter's here."

Booger started onto the field, dropping the two full cups of Gatorade, one on the ground, one into the lap of a sweaty first string defensive end whose white home-game pants blossomed an orange stain from his crotch to his knees. The mountain of a child stood abruptly, took one mighty step toward his oblivious attacker and shoved him from the back so Nathan slid onto the field on his face as the kicker kicked the ball, releasing the eager players from their stances. They ran toward Peter.

Peter, seeing the onslaught, crumpled also onto his knees. The two Aspies, nephew and uncle, looked like they were praying devoutly to the Mecca of the other.

"Dammit," Paula said under her breath. "I don't want to do this." But I was already up and over the railing, stepping down onto the bench between two third-stringers.

I was beside Nathan and hefting him to his feet with my left arm around his chest. A one-armed restraint required much less paperwork. "Sit there," I said firmly and loudly enough for the bench to hear and make room for him. He obeyed immediately, still stunned.

Uncle Peter, however, was more like a turtle. When I went to lift him up he pulled his arms and legs in and went rigid. I carried him toward the stands, an arm under each of his crossed at the chest. Paula was waiting at the sidelines. When he saw her, his legs fell down to the ground, taking his weight and then I just had to keep my arm across his back, just like escorting a kid. I attuned myself to monitor the tension in his shoulders. Some Aspies don't like to be touched at all and others crave it.

I looked back to Nathan. Should I go get him too? If he left during a game he would be out for the season. He was not sitting on the bench where I'd left him. I scanned the sidelines, the bleachers. He wasn't there.

Then I looked to the field to see if he had made his way back out there, maybe looking for his uncle. And there he was, again on his knees. But this time, he was bracing himself under the weight of the kicker, who'd fallen awkwardly while trying to abort his kick-off. Nathan helped him to his feet then limped him off the field.

I continued along with his uncle. Booger would be fine. "Affenpinscher, bichon frise, Catahoula leopard dog, dachshund," Peter said.

"What the hell is he doing?" I blurted out, forgetting my rule not to curse in front of parents. Or at all.

I couldn't help it. He would lean forward and say, "Elk hound." Lean back and say, "Fox hound."

Forward: Great Pyrenees.

Back: Havanese.

"He's stimming," Paula said, "It's perfectly normal."

"I know it's normal, but what is he doing?" Stimming was self-stimulation. Some Aspies would flap their hands or clap or hum. Rocking was the most recognizable stim.

"Naming dog breeds," she said. "Alphabetically."

"Oh, I see," I said, rolling my eyes. Nathan listed obscure songs alphabetically. In fact, when I looked back at him on the sidelines he was rocking back and forth, and I imagined I could hear him: Always on my Mind, Born on the Bayou, Colour my World, Dancing Days.

I felt guilty, and I should have. It was a horrible thing to do. Here's what I told myself about it. I had learned more from mom in twenty minutes after the bake-sale beer, than I had in the previous twenty-or-so years. I felt like I'd really gained insight into why I was, figuratively, living in my parents' basement. More than I could have learned in four years of psychoanalysis.

On our following mother-daughter DVR date, she had been as reticent as the selective mute I'd had a couple of years ago, and that kid hadn't said a word since she saw her daddy kill her mommy when she was seven.

So I stopped by the liquor store on my way home from the gym. With the box of wine I had, I thought I could learn a little bit more, and maybe help Manny, during the Longhorn game. Manny was not necessarily a seeker, but if he had all of his abortion bucks back—or could save some in the future—he might be able to restore that old Camaro. And provide more family for me and a distraction for Mama.

The fake dog barked and Edna chirped, the coon version of a meow, and jumped onto the end table and up to my shoulders. "Hook 'em!" I shouted, the Texas equivalent of hello. Other Saturday Texas greetings include Guns Up, Gig 'em, and Wreck 'em; there were others, but I had never really paid that much attention. I was destined to go to the University of Texas from the beginning, although Mom did make a slight effort at the last minute to send me to University of Dallas, a Catholic University, until she read about the private school tuition costs.

She scratched Edna's head with one hand and gave me the horns with the other. "Watch your back, Ellie. Edna's a real pudge. She's just like her grandma. We're getting thick in our old age, aren't we, Eddie?"

"Where's Manny?"

"He's on his way. You brought wine? What's the occasion?"

"Well, not much of one if it's in a box," I said. "I didn't want Father 'Nugent' to be your supplier."

"Ellie, you shouldn't make fun of our foreign priests. God knows we are running out of the American ones. They're either going to jail or going to St. Peter as fast as we can import them." She took the wine and expertly popped the hole and extracted the nozzle. It reminded me of an experienced midwife, for some reason. "You better rinse those wine glasses, you know they're dusty."

I got three etched glasses from the hutch and rinsed them. Manny would have some wine although he would complain about it the whole time. Why couldn't I have bought beer? Why? Because Mama saw wine as sacramental, and she would guzzle it and spill her guts about the psychology of my emotionally enforced celibacy, I hoped, before she started spilling her guts puking up the cheap wine.

"I got the Ro-Tel in the Crock-Pot, sweetie. Call Manny on the carphone and tell him to bring some chips."

"Why'd you make cheese dip if there are no chips?" I asked.

"I have some, but—oh, shoot there he is," Manny's car chugged into the driveway.

"That doesn't sound good," I remarked, sticking my finger into the dip. "Damn, that's hot."

"Well, that's what you get, Miss Manners. He said his car was acting up. He's going to leave it here. I told him he could stay here or you'd drive him home and bring him back tomorrow for the early game. He can work on it here tomorrow."

"He can't fix anything. He should get fixed," I said, resurrecting our last argument, removing the chip clip from the bag of generic tortilla chips. "Just kidding, Mom," I preempted before she could smack me with either the dish towel or the fly swatter she held.

"What?" she said, obviously distracted. "You're right, it'll probably grow a pasture around it before he can do anything but have it towed." Outside Manny lifted his creaky hood.

"Like father, like son," I said. "Remember that time that big old Thunderbird got stuck in the mud out in Elgin?"

"That fool," she said. "That's just what your daddy was going to do. Leave it there."

"I was ready to."

"*You* were? I would have carried the both of you if I had to," she laughed and covered her face for a second with her towel. Would she cry that easily? Out of sadness or laughter?

Daddy had a temper. Not with us. He hardly ever yelled at another human. He really didn't have to; he was 6'7" with a lineless face like it was chiseled out of brown marble, a face that looked scarier when he was smiling than when he was scowling, because it was more suspicious.

Inanimate objects were more Daddy's targets. On the day of the John Deere acquisition, Mama and I had seen the destruction of the Toro on the front lawn. It was almost twenty-seven years ago, but I could still remember looking out the window and wanting so badly for the lawn mower to start that I would blow a little through my lips, making a motor noise every time he pulled the starter cord. "Please, please, please," I would think and Mama would whisper.

Mechanical devices cannot be intimidated to acquiescence, and Daddy was helpless when facing a gasoline or electrically powered device. After body slamming the mower onto the ground several times, he wrenched the blade loose and hacked the rest of it to pieces. When he left for the Western Auto, I helped Mama clean up the pieces, and that time she did laugh until she cried. "It's out of gas," she kept repeating loudly to the neighbors, who had been watching the conflict. Man versus machine.

If he'd had a lawn mower blade when the Thunderbird got stuck, we might not have made it. He'd tried for an hour to get it out while Mom and I had been trapped inside. Finally, with an uprooted fence post, Daddy beat it so badly that the insurance agent believed our roll-over story, and the car was totaled.

"This Ro-Tel is good. I'm going to send Manny to the store in my car to get some chips. Anything else?"

"You got money for cigarettes?"

"Would I even try to send my brother to the store without cigarette money?"

Manny was still leaning under his hood, looking perplexed.

"Hey," I said, smacking him on the butt. Basketball shorts, no underpants—not a good idea. "Did you bring your laundry?"

"Yeah," he smiled, but I could see the tension in his face.

"Don't worry, brother, we'll get it fixed. It's the Longhorns' opening tonight, though, and your family needs you."

"Thanks, sis," he slammed the hood, sat on it and looked at his knees.

"Tough day at the office, dear?" I teased.

"Nah, in the field all week." Manny was a roofer's estimator which meant, I inferred, that he was a fairly convincing liar. I also recognized that, in central Texas, May to October was not a pleasant time to be on someone's roof, even if you were just up there to make up lies.

"Tired?"

"Yeah, but I can't have my car broke."

"Well, we can't be out of tortilla chips when Mama has a Crock-Pot full of Ro-Tel," I handed him a twenty, then opened my wallet and pulled out another. "I've got a former student who may be able to help you out. You know him. Mikey."

"Jesus, Ellie. I hate that kid. He's so ADD, he chases his tail half the time."

"He won't charge you by the hour so don't fret." Of course we both knew that Manny wouldn't be paying for it anyway.

"Now go get some real chips, Tostito's, and whatever else you need. Like condoms." He took the forty dollars. "I brought wine."

"Really?"

"Yeah, Mom was a hell of a lot more fun after a couple of beers. The blood of Christ ought to turn her into a three ring circus."

"Can I get some cigarettes?"

"Will you be nice to my cat?"

"Fuck your cat."

"Not even Edna is safe from your perversion? Get back by the time the second quarter starts or I'll report my car stolen." He crawled into the driver's seat, checking his back pocket for his wallet right before he sat down. More Mom training. You've got to have your driver's license. "Love you, brudder," I said, but I waited until he'd closed the door and started the car, tuning the radio to classic stoner rock.

"Alrighty, the chili is done," Mom said when she heard the tinny arf-arf-arf as I walked back in.

"Mom, chili? Geez, it was 105 degrees today."

"Some people believe that eating warm foods and drinking hot tea will make you cooler."

"Yeah, stupid people believe that, and I'm not going to drink any hot tea. That's clear proof that you fought for the Union in a previous life. Tea comes in two varieties: sweet and unsweet."

"Ellie, you'd bitch with your tit caught in a ringer," Mom said. It was an old saying and obviously made no sense.

"You got some hot tea, there?" I asked playfully.

"No, Ellie, I didn't want to be rude. This is your lovely cabernet blend."

Yeah, cabernet blended with rubbing alcohol. "It's a real celebration. This is the year. Last national championship was in, what? 2005?"

"Until this year," Mom toasted.

"Amen, sister," I clinked her glass.

"How'd the boys do this week?" Mama asked as we settled onto the couch for the pregame show, meaning our Savages' away game.

"Good, beat Lago Vista."

"Anymore breakdowns on the field?" I couldn't remember if I'd told her about Nathan and his uncle or if maybe she'd heard it at the church.

"No one told me anything. If our trainer had broken down in a Muslim prayer session again, I'm sure I'd have heard all the details."

"I'm sorry I missed that first game. It sounds darned entertaining."

"Not that much," I explained. "My kiddo, Nathan, went back to the field with just some grass burns on his nose."

"And the crazy that wondered onto the field?"

"He wasn't a streaker, Mama, he was just lost. It was my trainer's uncle; he didn't realize the game had started."

"Here's Mack Brown from last night," she interrupted, pointing the remote at the TV. Edna crawled into her lap. "Have you been neglecting my grandcat?" she asked me.

"Probably, it's been a tough week. We have a new instructional assistant, and my autistic kid was in In-School-Suspension for three days last week so it was like re-teaching him a whole new world when he came back." Mom was only pretending to listen, reading the closed captioning as I recounted my week. "And my sex kitten was given two weeks of Saturday school for using the softball dugout as a kissing booth. Of course, there was the poop-flinging episode, and, despite my lackadaisical efforts, Munch was given a whole week of ISS starting Monday. It'll be like a vacation for me, though."

Edna chirped for sympathy—not for me but for her—and rammed her head into mom's neck and flopped on her back for some rubbin'-lovin', she knew she couldn't count on constant attention once the game started.

———————

Periodically, Edna visited the porch but finding no cicadas, she came back in, expertly pawing the screen door open each time. She made sure to go out and check every few minutes, and she was out there when Manny finally came back during half-time.

"Come 'ere, kitty-cat. Watcha' got there? You found a bug?" He came in carrying Edna on his shoulders, a grocery bag and a 6-pack of Miller Lite. "See, sis, I remembered to get paper instead of plastic. I can be nice to your cat."

"Thanks, Manny. You sure were gone a long time, you missed half the game." I followed him into the kitchen.

"I got to the HEB just as Crystal was going on break so I grabbed a Whataburger with her," he said.

"Crystal's my age! God, Manny. I should have called the police. Don't you have any standards?"

"Not many. As a matter of fact, I wanted to ask about your date at the football game last week. Steamy hot, you were all over him," Manny said, successfully changing the subject. He opened a beer and jumped up to sit on the counter. Mom was piqued enough to leave the half-time talk to come into the kitchen.

"You didn't tell me you had a date, Ellie," Mom said, filling her glass again.

"I didn't, Manny's just showing his butt. You know what I do for a living, Manny, do you think you should be making fun of people with special needs?"

"Jesus, you do it all the time! You probably already have a nickname for him. Besides, sweetheart or hotstuff."

"Don't use the Lord's name in vain, son." The game came back on in the living room, and I looked longingly toward it. "There will be no television until you explain yourself, young lady," Mom said, smiling as if she were joking, but I knew better.

Manny looked satisfied and swigged his beer. "That was not my date, as I'm sure you know, brother. It was Nathan's uncle I told you about, the 'crazy man' on the field. My student with autism, his uncle has the same disorder."

"You should have seen it. Ellie picks this guy up and hauls him off the field, just like she does Edna. She always talks about wrestling these kids and I didn't believe it, but damn, what a bad-ass. He's rocking like Rain Man. It was awesome." Manny drained his beer and opened another.

"It wasn't awesome. The man was scared. He had some sort of anxiety attack."

"She stayed snuggled up next to him for the rest of the game," he reported. Mama raised her eyebrows at me.

"I did. Just hear the whole story, okay. Peter walked out onto the field right at kick-off, and he looked up and sees the ball falling out of the sky at him, and those big boys rushing at him. He ducked and covered. It looked funny, but it was very practical. Then the crowd is yelling and the whistles are blowing and those boys are huddled over him cursing and calling him names. Then this giantess picks him up. Peter was traumatized, I'm sure."

"Peter?" Mom asked. "So you had to therapatize him for the rest of the game?"

"Maybe something like that. I was sitting with Nathan's mom before he came, so it would have been weird for me to move once Peter got there. He was pretty shaken up. He's a veterinarian, see, and when he gets upset he names dog breeds," I started, but seeing the way they were looking at me I just stopped.

"He's a doctor?" Manny asked skeptically.

"Yeah, he owns a vet clinic with his sister, Nathan's mom. In fact, during the game, she gets a call about a dying cat and had to leave to go to the clinic."

"Why didn't he go?"

"I don't know," I said opening the chips and scraping the skin off the cooling dip. "Apparently, he doesn't like cats that much. And he's not good in a crisis, Paula said." Manny sputtered, laughing.

"So you two love birds got some alone time?" Mom was now in on it.

"Yep," I just went along with it. "By the end of the game, we were engaged, which was only natural after what we did during half-time."

"The horizontal mamba," Manny said.

"The mamba is a snake, you boob, it's the mambo and we did it vertically, standing under the bleachers."

"Ellie!" Mom said, shocked, but she was smiling, even as she was sipping her wine.

"Conduct unbecoming a teacher, I'd say, sister. You'll never be a Sister that way."

"I'm not a nun. Whoever said I wanted to be a nun? What if I had been on a date with Peter? What would be wrong with that? What if I even had sex with him? I'm 32 years old," suddenly I was crying, realizing I was 32 years old. I abandoned the chips. "I'll watch the game in my room. Mikey will be here in the morning to fix your car. It'll be done in time for you to drive Mom to mass."

"Don't be like that, Eloise, your brother was just playing."

"My brother? What about you?" I took a deep breath, Mama may be a barrel of monkeys with some wine, but it turned out I was a sad and angry drunk. "I know. I'm sorry. I just get, I don't know. Maybe lonely?" I lifted the sleeve of my t-shirt to wipe my eyes.

"Don't be ridiculous. You have a loving family, a nice trailer home, a job where you're successful and valued," Mom was sincere; she really believed that I had everything I should need. And what was wrong with her thinking that? I'd thought so too. Until when? When did it change? Maybe it was when I sat with my arm around an adult man while watching a danged football game for the first time. Or maybe knowing what my brother had and wasted. My box of wine had backfired.

Manny snorted dramatically, sucking the snot into his throat. He spat and it plopped into the trash can. "I can't believe that you have found so many women who will let you stick that tongue in their mouths," I said, trying to join in his attempt to leaven the mood or at least change the subject.

"You ever had a tongue in your mouth?" He asked.

"I've had my own in there for 32 years."

"And no others I'll wager," he laughed and put down his beer.

"No, Manny, you sick pervert, I can see what you are thinking." But before I

108

could run, he'd launched himself off the counter. He was at me, laughing and snorting his sinuses again.

"I'm hot for teacher," he sang, and caught me around the wrist, pulling me to him. I thought of all the restraints I had been trained to do. All the boys bigger than Manny that I'd had to wrestle to keep others safe. All the violent, angry girls wielding scissors or mini-blades from hand held pencil sharpeners. But I was never running away from them.

So I went into the situation, not around or away from it. I turned around to face Manny. "I brought my pencil," he said, pushing himself against me, I raised my knee into his groin.

"Kids, y'all stop it right now," Mom said, but too late, Manny was falling and groaning, and taking me down with him. I hadn't hit him hard, just hard enough.

When we hit the ground, his arm was wrapped around my waist, his other hand was holding his manparts. He licked my face, and I rolled away from him into my mother's feet. She was swatting at us with the broom like a pair of stray dogs. "Give me something to write on," Manny said, and pulled my head back by my hair and crammed his tongue into my mouth.

9

Krista was on her knees with rubber gloves and a box of Lysol scrubbing wipes when I walked in.

"Sorry I'm late. I had to take my brother to work." Manny's car was a little more broken than we'd anticipated. Mikey wasn't able to get it fixed last Sunday, but Tuesdays were his day off and he expected to get it fixed by the end of the day. "If I have to spend one more morning with that brother of mine, I might become an only child." I had told Krista what had happened last Saturday night, and she failed to see why it was traumatic.

"It's not like he was trying to rape you or anything, your Mom was right there," she'd said. "You probably swap more spit with him when you take a swig of his beer. You two slid out the same vagina, for God's sake."

"So the janitorial staff fails again?" I asked, kneeling beside her.

"No, they put the trash can over the spot. Disappeared like magic."

"I'll finish this, I'm sorry you got left with it."

"It's okay. I've cleaned so much dried blood off the floor in my time I've developed a theory. I really think that blood from a person who is getting the crap beat out of them has a worse smell. And not because of the crap, that's just figurative."

"Yeah, like when you stress-sweat. Adrenaline," I said. I looked at the pinkening blood. "Of all the ass-whippings in the history of the world, this one was the best. Most deserved, and most, just...satisfying."

"Trix is smarter than she looks," Krista said, pulling out a new behavior log for her clipboard and bouncing her butt against the file cabinet door to close it. "You see the way she rolled Munch on top of her when Officer Hotty came in? I bet she takes charge in the bedroom."

"Krista! We do not discuss our students' sex lives," my voice was light, but I was serious, it was literally the last topic in the world I wanted to discuss, ever. "I'm glad she was able to save Munch's mom the trouble of making him swallow screws or drink Drano for this trip to the emergency room. God, poor kid. As much of a poophead as he is, when you think of the whole story, you can't help feel sorry for him."

"I can. Pulling down Trixie's skirt and screaming 'she-male'? That's unforgivable. Oh, by the way, you're in big trouble with The Whale's mom," she said.

"What did I do now?"

"I saved the message for you," she hit the speaker phone button and played the voicemail for me while I finished up the floor and washed my hands.

"Miss Warden, this is Mrs. de los Santos," she began, then cleared her throat. I wondered if she had intended that contrast in our titles. Considering the life she had created, perhaps I shouldn't fret about wanting a family.

"My son came home yesterday and reported that during your social skills class," you could hear her implied quotation marks around social skills, "you chose to exhibit some very poor social skills, indeed. As you know, I hope, my son is in your care," (quotation marks around care), "because of his suicidal tendencies."

"Isn't that a band?" I asked Krista. "Suicidal Tendencies?"

"Maybe. Ask Booger."

"It is appalling, therefore, that you would be callous enough to play a game of Hangman. How dare you make light of my son's—" I hit delete.

"I can't believe they let that little poop-flinger out of juvie already. A game of Hangman? Really? Get a life, lady. She makes it sound like I gave him a rope and a chair."

"And a field trip to the park. Oh, Whale, look at that tall tree! Can you hold this rope and chair for me?"

"Then we could use him as a piñata," I started to laugh and still had my head lolled and tongue protruding when Jacky walked in. "Hey, Jacky, you're here early," I said, casual conversation to right myself and put the trashcan back on the ghost of the bloodstain. Of all the kids, even Trixie, she'd been the most upset by the fight the day before. I hugged her. "You need to process some stuff?"

She was already heaving in my arms, grabbing fistfuls of my shirt, sobbing. "Wow, you are really troubled by the kids' fighting, huh?" Jacky wailed louder and fell to her knees, dragging me with her. I looked at Krista, but she looked more terrified than she had during yesterday's blood bath. After several minutes, Jacky was able to say,

"Daddy's gonna' kill me. That's no metaphor or hyperbole, Miss Warden."

"What happened, angel? Tell me everything so we can fix it up."

"I'm pregnant."

Thank God we had sat down. I felt my vision go black and fuzzy like an Elvis painting. "You must be so scared," I said by rote.

Her sobs peaked and then ebbed. Krista, having learned the nature of the problem, was less terrified. I realized, sadly, that Krista would be much better at this than I would. So I held Jacky, and pleaded telepathically for Krista to take over.

"Come on, let's get Miss Warden over to the couch. She's an old woman." Krista pulled Jacky up and led her to the couch, and I grabbed a chair and pulled it close so I could hold Jacky's hand. "Who's the father, Jacky? Are you going to get some support there?" Krista handed her a tissue.

She stiffened, her hand becoming rigid in mine. That was not the question I would have started with. I'd already assumed that the father was either a complete mystery to her or her own father. "I don't know," Jacky said, in a voice that told me she was lying—and she wanted us to know it.

"How far along are you, sweetie, do you know that?"

"I don't know. Just a couple of months, or not quite yet."

"I'm so glad you asked for support so early. You're being very brave, sweetie," I said.

"Yeah, so we have some time to decide what to do," Krista said, and now I stiffened. Time for what? I wanted to ask, but I knew. I wondered if I could be excommunicated for listening to a conversation planning an abortion. I began to say the Rosary, counting the prayers off on my fingers. "What do you see as your options?" Krista asked.

"I don't know. I just found out. But, oh my God, when Daddy—or my baby daddy—finds out. I don't know what I'll do. I don't know what they'll do."

She seemed pretty comfortable with the baby-daddy title, I thought. It was part of her world's vernacular, I guessed.

"You can't hide it forever," I said.

Krista looked at me with wide eyes. Her lips tense, "If you decide to terminate the pregnancy, though, you'll need to make that decision soon."

"Jacky," I interrupted, "I'm going to write you a pass to the nurse. I want you to go down there, wash your face, calm down, and come back when you're feeling better. I'll call your teachers and let them know that you'll be in the unit until further notice." The other kids were due in ten minutes, and I had to make a game plan with Krista.

"We can't facilitate an abortion for this child," I told Krista as soon as Jacky left the room. "We could be held accountable for that forever. Think it over. Jacky is 40 years old and barren, and she sues us because we advised her to abort her child, ruining her uterus, thus making her life trivial and without merit."

"You want your tax dollars to pay to raise Jacky's child and then pay to incarcerate or execute him? She's mentally ill, probably pregnant with the product of incest, and you don't think that will make her life worthless?"

"We can't be held accountable for that in a court of law."

"Jesus, Ellie, who are you today? This is a child we're talking about."

"I know. It is a child we are talking about, and I won't advise that it be killed," I said hotly.

"Give me a break, Ellie. You can fall back on your Catholicism like you've got iced holy water in your veins, but this is more than a philosophical question, or a matter of the law. This is the time to be a salad bar Catholic, pick the good stuff, but skip the nuts.

"You might hold onto your holiness like a security blanket so you don't have to face the wide wicked world of real life, but Jacky's already there," Krista stopped abruptly when the kids walked in, but the tension was clear even to our narcissists. They sat down in our group formation quietly and waited for the adults to begin.

————————

"Where is everyone?" Becca asked when she came in. She always came in late, because it was harder to count the lockers while they had students opening them. She waited outside until the tardy bell rang. By the time she arrived we were circled up for goal-setting for a Terrific Tuesday, and debriefing our melee on Monday.

We were a small group today. Jacky was at the nurse's, Munch was in ISS again after taking the fall for yesterday's fight, Brian had been kept home with the sniffles, and The Whale had been kept home on suicide watch due to the scandalous Hangman episode. That left Trevor, Trixie, Nathan, and now Becca.

I told her the accounting of where everyone was, and her only response was, "I'm the only girl, and I can't sit in the middle." Yes, it would be disproportionate.

"Should I sit with you?" Krista asked.

"Hold up there a minute, girlie. What the hell am I?" Trixie challenged.

"Well, a lady certainly doesn't use that kind of language," I chided.

"I'm a 21st century woman, Miss Warden," Trixie said. Becca sat next to her, making a patterned array.

"That will be a demerit, little lady," I told Trix.

"Great, so that brings me to 862 demerits after yesterday, right?"

"You are such a bad-ass, Trix, I had no idea," Twitch said.

"Jacky!" Krista said, and I turned to see her. She'd been gone only 15 minutes, and she looked 15 times worse than when she left.

"There's nowhere for me to sit without wrecking the pattern," Jacky smiled.

"How are you feeling?" Trixie asked, scooting over, "and you will make three." She patted the couch. Jacky's face looked like a waxy mask.

"Three girls in a row today," Becca said sprightly.

"Should you go home?" Nathan asked. "You might be contagious, and even if you don't cough, sneeze, or vomit—or expel any other sort of bodily fluid, you are emitting contaminated breath from your respiratory system."

"I told your friends that you visited the nurse's office," I explained to Jacky. "Maybe you're just sniffley. Brian is at home with a cold today," I added helpfully.

"No, I've been crying," she said. She looked at me then Krista, took a breath and said, "I'm going to have baby."

"What a surprise," Booger said without emotion.

"Oh my," said Becca, tapping her head, belly, head, belly.

"Holy Ghost," said Trixie.

"Gobsmacked!" Twitch said.

"Who decided that I have special needs?" Nathan asked, and he was angry. "I don't think I'm so different from everyone else. I've read a lot about Asperger's syndrome. It's diagnosed through symptoms. No, through surveys of your symptoms as assessed by parents and teachers and a psychologist who knows you for no longer than three hours," Nathan exploded in a vomitous commentary.

"What triggered that tirade, Nathan?" I asked tiredly. Even still without Munch, The Whale, and Brian, it had not been a Terrific Tuesday, although it had beat the hell out of the crap slinging of the previous week. Jacky, of course, had been humping my leg all day, figuratively, of course. She'd told me how the nurse had shown her the diagram of the baby's development, and started a short film on the progression of a pregnancy when she decided she was well enough to return to class and announce her condition to the class. I wondered if it had given her enough courage to tell her daddy. Although I'd never been out of Texas, I was sure this school nursing technique would have been intolerable in, say, Massachusetts or Oregon.

"In AP biology today," Nathan began, and I tried hard to listen, but I'd already heard the story, which the teacher had screeched at me very loudly through the speaker phone while I lunched on the last tin of tuna in the food stash. "I wasn't trying to be rude, I was just pointing out that his theory of creationism has a few flaws."

"So you don't think you were disrespectful at all?"

"Well, eventually."

"Tell me exactly what you think you shouldn't have said."

"Just that he shouldn't be a biology teacher if he didn't believe in actual science."

"I'm sure that did set him off a little. What do you think you should do to heal the relationship?" I'd said the same words to Munch when I'd been called down to the ISS room.

He'd thrown a hand weight through the wall and was threatening the ISS teacher, Coach Davis, with the heaviest dumbbell he could lift, which wasn't that heavy because in spite of his portliness he was kind of a wimp. I'd gotten the "weapon" away from Munch easily, and then questioned Davis about why the detention/suspension room looked like Gold's Gym. It turns out the athletes spend a lot of time in ISS, and the day can't be wasted, after all.

Coach Davis had told me I was welcome to work out in this secondary weight room any day after 4:00. He'd even assign me a locker to keep a change of clothes in. I had a creepy feeling that he'd be rubbing my change of panties along his stubbled face. I told him that I had a locker in the girls' locker room, and I told him how it had come in handy very recently. I let him laugh at my expense so he wouldn't make me take Munch back with me.

To fix the situation, Munch had decided that he'd purchase a framed poster of some athletic felon and hang it over the hole in the wall. Coach had agreed and they'd shaken hands on it. I was back in the classroom to hear more ranting calls from Whale Mom and then the science teacher and finally the principal, who had heard about Munch's redecoration of the weight room.

"Are you listening?" Nathan prodded me into the present, recounting his biology class fiasco.

"No, sweetie, I wasn't. I'm sorry. It was very astute of you to notice. Good job picking up on my facial cues."

"See that's the thing. It's not that I can't read faces and emotions. It's just that I don't really care much. Nobody is interested in others unless it impacts them, but I have an excuse so I don't have to pretend to care like most people do—or don't do," he looked at me pointedly, but not quite at my eyes. "Asperger's is just a label that parents use to excuse their children's behaving like they're smarter than everyone else because they actually are smarter than everyone else. Wikipedia says, 'Pursuit of specific and narrow areas of interest is one of the most striking features.' But I don't have an unnatural obsession with B-side songs, it's just a subject so fascinating that I think most ignorant people would be interested if they had the patience to get educated. I mean think of the songs as sort of throw-away songs. Space fillers—but the artists are fallible, they don't know what their fans will like, really. For example—"

"You have some interesting coping skills, don't you think, though?" I interrupted.

Angie Bennett

"No, I just list songs. I learned that from my uncle. Everybody has coping skills. I think it's a pretty healthy one. Some people, when faced with a real or imagined crisis, may pray or become violent or have a cigarette, a drink, or take drugs."

Jacky said, "But you just look crazy, no offense. You don't look at people and you rock and you're just weird most of the time."

"And we're not all weird? You make a show of licking your armpit to give a male-girl an erection? That makes both of you crazy. What's a little rocking compared to armpit licking, or Trixie getting off on it for that matter?"

"Yeah, that explains it," Twitch agreed, "picking your nose excessively seems like at least as big a special need as having a healthy sexual appetite, being a lesbian trapped in a boy's body. Or even The Whale; he's not disabled, he's just a crap-stain, Becca orders her world with counting, and Brian whacking it all the time. Who doesn't?" Perhaps I was the only one who noticed that Trevor had left himself off the list of excused craziness.

"What about Austin?" Becca asked.

"Oh, that dude's crazy," several students said, I couldn't even determine who to redirect with my typical, "We

124

don't say retarded, crazy, or stupid." At least not while the children are here.

My phone rang. Not my desk phone, which was always put on Do Not Disturb for group processing time, but my iPhone. No one ever called it, not even my mom, so it took me several seconds to even recognize it as mine. I dug it out of my purse just as it stopped ringing. It was a school number. Obviously someone needed to reach me pretty badly. When my desk phone was on DND, it went straight to voicemail, and the message light was blinking. A lot.

I picked up the handset and called my mailbox. Mr. White, the principal, was agitated. "I have reports of a student with a gun on the lower floor, near ISS, and I wanted to see which of your freaks was not accounted for. We're calling a Code if I don't hear from you." I threw Krista my keys and mimed locking the door, but before she took even a step in that direction, the overhead P.A. system blared 4 short beeps, and a calmer sounding Mr. White said, "Teachers, this is a Code Red. Please follow the Code Red procedure until further notice."

Krista was frozen. "Lock the door," I prompted too loudly. My chest was tightened, and I could feel the distinct pulse in my neck. I looked at my kids, some had been lounging on the floor on bean bags, the afternoon group being less formal than morning goal-setting, but now they were crammed together on the couch. Nathan rocking, Becca tapping nose-chest-nose-chest, Twitch restraining his vocal tics, causing his physical tics to be almost violent in his head-smacking, eye-rolling frenzy. Trixie and Jacky sat holding hands looking panicked. I remembered, finally, to hang up the phone.

I counted them. Five. Brian was at home, The Whale on hangman's watch. That's six and seven. Munch.

I handed Krista a laminated sheet of red paper with bold black letters, the Code Red Procedural. "I've got to go get Munch," I said. "I mean Austin. He's in ISS."

"He might be roaming the halls with a gun," Nathan suggested.

"Of course, he isn't. In fact, probably no one is. It's probably just a drill, but he must be scared."

"Don't leave, Ellie," Krista said. She was almost crying. I grabbed her by the wrist and took her with me toward the door.

"You cannot act like this. The kids can't see that you are scared. Read the procedures, keep away from the door and windows, and I will call you when I get to the ISS room. I can't bring Munch back through the halls, though. I'll have to stay there." I thought for a second. What else do you tell someone at a time like this? It's just a drill. Our school gets a grade from Homeland Security. You gotta' follow the rules. "Don't open the door for anyone. The Code Red password is 'gopher.' If anyone says they're here to evacuate you, they'll give the password. Otherwise, stay here.

"You'll be fine, Krista. Tell the kids they'll be fine. Later, we'll go to a bar and smoke cigarettes and drink beer and watch the news footage, and recite B-side songs if necessary. Give me the keys, I'll lock the door from the outside."

The halls were quiet, quieter than they ever were during the school day. The door separating the unit from A-hall, magnetized like the stairwell doors, was only shut during Codes or Code Drills. It was stiff, untried. I wished I had worn jeans instead of picking this day to wear a dress. Even though it was supposed to be fall, our 100 degree streak was still strong so I had put on the coolest clothes I owned. Not practical for restraints, but comfortable. With Munch out of the room, I thought I only had The Whale to consider and I'd made a commitment not to restrain him again, and I'd thought myself home-free when he'd not shown up for school again today.

I had to hike up my dress and use my knee to slide the door open wide enough to scoot through. It slid closed, clanking and echoing down the hall. If there was a shooter out there, he'd certainly be able to find me.

The stairway doors were more exercised and I had no trouble letting myself in to get to the first floor. Once I reached the ground floor, the ISS room would be just three doors down.

I stopped at the stairwell door to listen, and then the fire alarm started. It had always puzzled me that the fire alarm flashed blinding light and sounded a deafening siren. If you want people to get out of a burning building, why ensure first that they can't see or hear?

But I could hear. Or feel. Above me the hallway doors all opened at once, quaking the whole ceiling above me. Of course a fire alarm would trump the possible shooter lockdown. "Hail Mary, full of grace, the Lord is with Thee," I began.

The stairwell door opened easily, and I closed it quietly behind me. "Fuck you, fuckers!" I heard a voice screaming down the hall, barely audible, though, above the Wamp! Wamp! Wamp! of the fire alarm. I froze, and pressed myself close against the wall as if I could hide there. I was 6'1" and sturdily built, not likely to blend in with a pale green wall, but I sidled along like a Scooby-Doo character.

The alarm blared, but I heard the tinkling, tinny sound bounce off my left foot, like a cannon-shot through my body. It was a bullet casing. "Dead! Dead. This is the end!" I heard far to the right, into the center of the school, and then a steady four pops.

I ran for the ISS door and slammed my body into it. It was unlocked, but I was already yelling. "Austin? Austin! Gopher. I'm Miss Warden. Gopher," as I tried the knob. Someone hit me as soon as I walked in the room. A full body check, and we hit the ground.

11

He had knocked me into a puddle of blood, and I skidded with him riding on top of me like a sled. His head was sunk into my belly, and I could feel his face, wet with tears or blood. Coughing out sobs, and my name, he groped at me. I'd taught Chandler in freshman English. He was a good student. I couldn't believe he would do this.

"Chandler, are you okay? Are you hurt?" and he began to scream. Rising to his knees, he concentrated all of his weight on my left thigh, and I reflexively pushed him off. He fell back into the puddle and slid into the door, knocking it closed. With him off of me, I could see the room. It was bathed in blood, and gobs of tissue clung to one wall, but the room was still miraculously ordinary. The four chairs sat neatly behind study carrels, with the occupants slumped onto their desk tops. A couple of chairs were knocked over, the occupants spilled onto the floor, and the students' blood pooled around them. That's six. None of them had Munch's stringy greasy hair.

"Where's Coach?" I asked.

"He's gone." He pointed to the corner where the coach was still huddled, his face now just a bloody empty space. "They're all gone." Seven.

"Did you do this, Chandler. Oh God, why did you do this?"

"It wasn't me, I didn't do it."

"Who?" I asked skeptically. Then we heard the blam, blam, blam. "Lie down. Stay here."

"Don't leave me Miss Warden," he grabbed hold of the skirt of my dress and allowed me to pull him along through the blood.

"How many are there?"

"Just that one."

"Austin?"

"I don't know. He had hair, and a—" he pointed at his mouth.

"How did you—" but I couldn't say survive, because we hadn't yet. Again, a gunshot, shattering glass, screams, more gunshots. "Lie down. Act dead." I closed the door on him lowering himself into a pool of blood. I locked the door behind me and headed toward where I'd last heard the shots.

Passing classrooms, I saw that the rectangular windows running down the doors had been shattered. I stuck my face into one. "Gopher," I said first. "Are y'all okay?"

"Mostly," I heard Mrs. Wyndham answer weakly. "He was shooting through the window at us."

"Anyone called out? 911? Police? Parents?" I asked, but I heard shots again ahead of me, and didn't stay to hear the answer. "Austin?" I called loudly, but gently, I hoped.

Turning the corner, I saw him, just a glimpse of his limp brown hair before he ducked into an alcove for the water fountain. "Austin, honey? Are you hurt? Sweetie, there's someone in the school hurting people. You need to come somewhere safe with me, angel, I'll take you to safety," I said, as sweetly as I could. I could hear my voice shaking. "I heard shots this way. You need to come back toward me."

I could see him. He looked out at me. Blood was smeared across his face, and he had a long gash down his right arm. Probably from where he'd rested his arm against the broken window-glass to shoot inside the classroom. "You saw him?" he asked.

"No, but I heard him. You're already hurt, let me take you out this way. Most of the kids are outside." His right hand moved behind him; I couldn't tell if he was ditching the gun or tucking it into his pants. Either way, he couldn't let me see it. Not yet. "There's a good boy, let's go," and I walked confidently and quickly toward him. "This way," I said, grabbing his left arm. "We've got to hurry before he comes back. How did you get hurt, have you been shot, why weren't you in lockdown with everyone else? Did you see him?" I slammed my words at him to keep him mentally off balance while I dragged him behind me.

"No," he said, "I didn't see him," but he didn't get to finish his lie. I knocked his feet out from under him with my right foot while pulling him off balance with his uninjured arm. He fell heavily onto his back, and I was sitting on his chest, pinning his arms to his body by squeezing my knees together. I could feel the blood from his gashed arm seeping through my dress and even my underwear.

"Where's the gun? Who is with you?" I shouted in his face. "Where are the others? Tell me."

"No, no. Just me," he answered and then began to cry. Until then I hadn't realized how dead-eyed he had looked during our whole exchange. I wondered if he'd thought the same about me. He

133

was not a small boy, but he was not struggling except for his sobbing underneath me.

"Why did you do this?" I shouted louder than necessary and closer to his face than was comfortable. When he reeled in reaction, I flipped him over, and easily pulled the gun from his back pocket. I knew nothing about guns. Didn't know how to tell if it was loaded, let alone unload it. I sheltered his body with mine and then skidded the gun away from us along the polished tile floor. I pulled out my cell phone, and hit the call back button from principal's missed phone call. Ten minutes before. Only ten minutes.

"White!" he shouted.

"Ellie Warden. I have the shooter. We're outside classroom 110, Polson's room. There's a gun in the floor. Send someone in. Get me out of here," and then I cried. "Call my Mama, get me out of here."

"I can't breathe," Munch said into my ear, my whole body committed to immobilizing him.

"I don't care, sweetie. I actually could not care less at all." Then the police were there, lifting me, then him. "He's the one. Just this one. The ISS room, several dead, a kid's still in there,"

134

and I tried to run, but they held me, still unsure.

"I'm sorry. I'm sorry," Munch cried, collapsing, and they let me go. "Chandler! Chandler!" I screamed, running through the halls. Walk on the right, keep to the right, I heard my inner teacher voice prompting. Walk in the halls. I unlocked the door and he fell into me again. I hugged him, roughly, quickly, and headed him out the side door.

All the kids were in the building, locked down, and I expected that it would be quiet outside. They'd called their parents, though, and the police, and the media had heard, and they were all there. The two of us, blood soaked, and screaming, holding each other up, and pulling each other down in turns. Chandler and I hurled ourselves at and through the door of the building.

Finally, we fell onto the grass and did not try to rise again. Yelling, they were all yelling.

"What happened?"

"Who are you?"

"Is this the shooter?"

And then I heard someone, "Move, that's my son. Chandler." His mom was then beside him, holding him, and I ran back toward the building. After asking,

"You got him?" But there were more parents. More questions.

"Ellie! Ms. Warden, please. Where's my son?"

"Dr. Harmon, I don't know. I'm going to get him."

"Is he hurt? My God, you are covered in blood."

"No, I wasn't with him. Not with my class—I'm going back for my kids. Stay here."

But as I entered, someone, somewhere, disabled the fire alarm, and I was deafened now by the silence as I ran back into the building, up A stairwell and to my classroom. I heard the slapping footsteps of those damn plastic Crocs echoing my steps. Dr. Harmon. Who could blame her?

"Krista, let's go. Krista! Crap. Gopher. Effing gopher," I screamed pounding on the door, my face stuck to the window. And she opened the door. The kids were clustered around her, all hanging onto the fire drill rope. "Let's go."

"Nathan," she said, stricken, pointing back into the room. "The noise."

"I got him," Peter said, passing me up, startling me. The wrong Dr. Harmon. The wrong plastic shoes slapping behind me.

"Go, let's go," Trixie yelled.

"We're all going together," I said, "Nathan's uncle has him." Peter picked

Nathan up and balanced the kid on his hip; Nathan curled his legs up so they wouldn't drag the ground.

I led them easily through the halls, the rest of the doors still locked tight, with only a very few pale faces peering uneasily through the rectangular windows in the doors.

In shock, hurt, scared, I took the same path out that I'd taken in, past the ISS room.

"Christ on roller skates, look at that," Trevor shouted, pulling the whole string of us toward the room. It was worse than I remembered. A nightmare. A horror. I was too tired to resist. I just let go. Let them go.

"No," Peter said, dropping Nathan onto the bloody skid marks I'd left before.

I went to Booger and lifted him, not in a restraint but a hug, and walked him into the hall. "I'm okay, Miss Warden. Just the noise," Nathan said, but he did not look up, did not look into the room. Peter was pulling the children out and putting each of them beside Nathan and me in the hall, placing their hands on the handles, which they allowed numbly. He brought out Jacky and Trix together.

Peter burst through the door into the sunlight, pulling on that rope like a sled dog, and finally dropped it and us. I herded them to the grass where Chandler and his mom still clung to each other.

Reporters surrounded them, firing questions. Parents yelled their children's names. "Did you see him?"

Loud, it was too loud. Feeling the vomit threatening in my throat, I stumbled out of the closing circle, and finally released as I approached the ag barn. No one here. I heaved and heaved, and then finally rested there in the swag of grass by the barn. It was quiet. Except for the roar in my ears.

Then, someone brought me a bottle of water, opened it for me, and knelt beside me. I took the bottle, looking at it, trying to remember what one did with such a thing. I leaned my head back and poured it on my face. "Thanks," I said. The person was in a suit. He took his jacket off.

"Here," he said handing it to me, and I used it to wipe across my face and neck with an extra good swipe at my nose. It smelled like a man. Like cologne and stale cigarettes, and sweat. "How'd you get out?" he asked.

"I just turned the boy over and got my kids," I said, not really understanding the question. "Over to the cops. The doors were open because of the fire alarm."

He turned away from me. "Can we get her miked up?" he asked. Then, to me, "Can you stand?" He helped me to my feet and back until I could rest against the rough brick of the building. A man came with a black box and wires. "Miss, can we put this microphone on you?" he asked.

A lady with short dark hair, beautiful green eyes, looked up into my face. "You are a mess, poor thing. You okay?" The crowd had found me.

I nodded. "Yes," I said. I saw the cameraman then, and I understood. Finally. "Will we be live?" I asked.

"Yeah, babe, that okay?" she asked.

"Yes, I need to tell them their kids are okay."

"Since you are wearing a dress, we're going to have to hang this pack on your panties, okay?" She held up the battery pack. She took the reporter's jacket from me and gave it back to him. "Hold this up to shield her, Jeff."

She lifted my dress and hung the pack on the waistband of my Hanes for Her. Her hands were smeared with blood when she brought them out. She wiped them on the guy's jacket.

"I don't want to scare people. If I'm all covered with blood," I started.

"We'll only shoot you from your neck up."

"Jeff!" the woman said harshly. "He means film you, sweetie, not shoot you. What's your name?"

"Ellie Warden," I said.

"Let's scoop it, Ellie," he said cheerily, but when the camera began to roll he looked grim. "I'm here with teacher Ellie Warden, the first teacher to bring students out of the building after the reported shooting here at Shoemaker High School. Ellie, can you tell me what happened in there?"

"No, I can't, but I can tell the parents that the shooter has been disarmed and is in custody."

"Do you know of any casualties?" Jeff asked.

"Yes, I've seen some dead. But the shooter has been subdued and your children will be evacuated from the building shortly." The black haired lady handed me a tissue, pointing to her nose; I wiped my face.

Jeff said, "You will need to go to the United Methodist Church at Pecan and Johnson. Most of the district buses will be running between here and there to deliver your students to you safely. Go to United Methodist on Pecan Street. That is the best way to be reunited with your kids." Then he turned to me, "Did you see the shooter?"

"Yes, the shooter is in police custody," I said.

"Ellie, Ellie," I heard a voice yell. The black haired woman tried to stop him, but he dragged her along with him, barreling toward me. "Ellie, thank goodness you're okay," he said looking at his hands.

"Dr. Harmon," I said.

"Peter," he said, his face leaning forward out of his neck like a dog balancing a teacup on its head. "Just Peter," he repeated, raising his eyes as high as my breasts and wrapping his arms awkwardly around my waist and pulling me to him.

With his being about five inches shorter than me, it must have given the appearance that he was burying his head in my chest and humping my leg. The black haired lady pulled him from his middle, backing him up off me.

"We're live," she said pointing to the camera.

"I know. Thank God, we're alive! Ellie, I'm so glad you're alive." He rammed into me again. The cameraman finally isolated Jeff in the shot, as he gave overly detailed directions to the United Methodist Church.

"Peter. We were on the news. See the camera? That was all on the news.

Now when they point the camera back this way, you can stand here beside her, but no hugging or talking, okay?" the black haired lady told him sternly. I nodded.

"No talking," I repeated.

"Not you. Him."

"Can I take you out to dinner? Thank you for saving Nathan," he continued to gush.

"All those people out there need to know their kids are safe. You've got to tell them," the lady told me. "You've got to be quiet," she told Peter.

He turned around to face forward with me, put his arm only very gently around my waist. "No hugging and no talking," he said to himself.

"We have Ellie Warden here, who seems like a hero, being the first to usher out a group of kids, one of which, we hear, was a witness to the shootings of at least six students and one teacher. Miss Warden, can you confirm that?"

"No, I think that is something for the police to confirm. What I can tell parents is that the precautions we took to keep your children safe worked very well," Peter squeezed me around the waist, and the battery pack, attached to my underwear, began a slow slide. The wire running up my back and under my arm to hook onto the front of my dress tightened.   The microphone pulled downward, making me stiffen, and Peter squeezed harder.

"I believe that only one classroom was breached by the shooter," and my panties, wet with blood and sweat, weighted down, finally slid past my hips, pulling the microphone clip from my dress. And the pack and the panties fell down.

No one could blame the cameraman for looking. Anyone would have. And that's what would make the news: my panties lying in the grass, blotched with victims' or perpetrator's blood and Peter's voice. "Oh, it's your lady-time."

"Mom, I don't think that my biggest worry right now is whether or not I have a date with a very odd short man. And he's not that short; I'm just freakishly tall," I yelled at Mom, then Manny's voicemail beeped. "Brudder, you need to come over and protect me from reporters and your mother," I tried to sound normal, but a sob leaked out at the end.

Mom's voice on the other side of the door made some words, but I couldn't process them. I was still in bed, or back in bed, having gotten up and prepared myself for school before I realized that it would surely be closed. Today? This week? I heard the word underpants and a pause so I guessed it was my turn to speak.

"I had to wash someone's brains out of my hair last night. I don't care who saw my panties."

"Everyone saw your panties."

I just sobbed. I was so tired. I couldn't. I didn't care. I'd watched it over and over on the news until it had lost its meaning for me. And I'd heard commentators from all over the country mock Peter endlessly. CNN played a clip of Jay Leno imitating Peter's lady-time comment and then the rocking and dog naming that had followed.

The reporters were still outside the house, parked along the two-lane highway, and all along the side of the road, clogging the driveway. Someone was on my porch, live on the news as they were knocking on my door. Then Krista was beside him, "Move it, asshole." Somehow, she'd made it through the melee without their catching on that she was also part of the story. I jumped out of bed to go rescue her from the mob.

"Don't let anyone in, I'm not even dressed," Mom protested.

"So go get dressed," I said.

Krista pounded on my door, and she was also on the news crying "gopher" at my door. I opened the door, and she fell into me. I thought of Chandler. Falling into me. Sliding into the blood. The Coach's brains on the wall.

I held onto her while she closed and locked the door. She took me to the couch, and we collapsed there together, crying. How do you do this?

How do you process this? How do we help each other through and then bring the kids through? "I need a drink," I said.

"It's 9:00 in the morning, Ellie, just recite some B side songs."

"I'm better at dogs," I said. Edna chirped at Krista.

"Holy smack. What kind of cat is that?"

"A hungry one, I don't think I fed her last night, and I know I haven't fed her today." I got up, reluctantly, slowly, my body more sore than I thought possible from ten minutes of anything. "This is Edna. She's a Maine coon. She didn't eat a baby or anything, she's supposed to be that size."

Edna followed me to the bowl, and chirped at me, thanking me for filling it. She was so grateful after my neglect, that I opened a can of wet food and gave her that too.

"What are we going to do?" Krista asked.

"I have no idea. I can't even imagine. I don't know that I can go back there."

"We have to return to normal. At some point."

"There is no more normal," I said. "I need to regress for a while. Be a kid, not take care of kids." My cell phone vibrated, traveling across the counter.

They must have published my phone number on the news along with my blood sodden underpants. "That thing's been ringing all night and all morning."

"Reporters?"

"I have no idea." Krista picked up the phone and accepted the call.

"We have no comment," she said tersely into the phone, and I wondered if she was imitating me. Did I sound like that?

"Ellie!" I heard a voice come through the phone, and Krista held it away from her head. "Thank God. I've been calling you all night and day."

"Who is this?" Krista asked, without getting her busted eardrum too close to the phone.

"Peter. It's Peter." Krista held the phone out to me, her eyebrows lifted in a question. I shook my head.

"Peter, this is Krista, I'm a friend of Ellie's. I'm sure you can imagine that Ellie is feeling a little—well, I mean, she is just in bad shape today."

"No, she's in great shape. She's very strong despite being so skinny. Just a few weeks ago she carried me off the football field."

"She doesn't feel like talking or seeing anyone today. Or tomorrow. Jesus, are you kidding me? She's seen dead kids, disarmed a school shooter and lost her panties on the national news." I walked out of the room, down the hall to the bathroom. I had to brush my teeth.

While I was in there, letting the water run, very eco-unfriendly, to drown out Krista's voice, I piled up the clothes I'd left on the floor the day before, and threw them on top of the laundry basket. At least I could wash clothes, or put them out so Mom could, and Manny would probably bring his too.

"There's a man at the door," Krista said.

"It's a reporter," I said, opening the door. The phone was gone from her hand.

"I don't think so. He's not wearing a shirt, and he parked a Camaro on your lawn."

"That's my brother, Manny. You can let him in. Even if he doesn't say gopher."

I went into my bedroom to fetch any wayward dirty clothes, trying to put together a full load.

"Sis," Manny said as soon as I entered the living room. He wrapped me and my laundry basket up in his arms. "I'm so glad you called," he said.

"God, Manny, stop having feelings, it's creeping me out."

"No, I mean, I'm glad you called. It's supposed to be 102 degrees today and I had four roof-top appointments. What better excuse could I have to get a day off work?"

"Glad I could help out," I said.

"I'm so sorry, Ellie," he said, more serious than I'd ever seen him. "But I'm so mother-fucking proud of you."

"Thanks, Manny," I squirmed out of his sweaty arms, "Why don't you have your clothes on?"

"I figured the reporters would be less likely to stick a camera in my face if I looked like some hillbilly."

"You could have kept your shirt on and looked perfectly Appalachian, I assure you," Krista said behind him.

"Who the hell is that?"

"Start my laundry, I've been traumatized," I said, giving him the hamper, and picking up Edna.

"I'm Krista," she said. "I'm her instructional assistant, media spokesperson, and social planner."

"Great, what will my mom have left to do without running Ellie's social life?"

"You mean ruining my social life." We stood awkwardly in the living room, Manny holding a basketful of dirty and bloody clothes, Krista trying hard to look normal despite having eyes so swollen from crying she looked Japanese, me in mismatched flannel pajamas holding a 30 pound cat. All of us intensely aware of the strangers with cameras at all the windows.

"How can we be having a conversation about whether or not I have a social life when we have six dead kids, a dead teacher, and two kids whose lives are ruined forever."

"Two?" Krista asked.

"Two thousand," I said, "but I was thinking of Chandler seeing seven people murdered, and Munch."

"Munch," Krista repeated. "Why didn't he kill Chandler?"

"Okay, well, I don't know who Chandler is, but I do know that my sister's clothes smell like a dirty hamster cage. So let's go get them in the washer," Manny said, heading to the laundry room.

"Chandler was interviewed on the Today show. He said Munch told him that he wanted someone to tell the story, and tell it right," I told her.

"So what's the story?"

"I'm not sure I can—can, say." I took a deep breath. I'd tell her as much as I could, quickly. "Munch pulled a gun out of his pants and killed two kids who jumped up to run. Called them cowards. There were five more students, he said he'd leave one alive, if they stayed in their seats. The coach begged for his life, said he'd tell the story, but Munch shot him in the face. Then he made a speech. You can watch Chandler tell it on the re-runs." I had to stop. I could see Munch standing there, his eye purpled from Trixie's beating, lip busted, telling his story.

"When he finished, he gave the kids a quiz, sort of, about his speech. They got an answer wrong and he shot them in the back of the head. Chandler was the last one left."

Mom came in, then, her hair brushed and make-up on, looking ready for mass, she was already talking, "It was just awful, that poor young man, I don't know how he'll ever have a normal life." She started the coffee. Was it time for mass? 9:00. Was it Sunday? I couldn't remember.

"Mom, this is Krista. Krista, this is my mother Frances Warden," I said.

"Who do you mean?" Krista asked. And I looked at her confused. Had I flubbed the introductions? But she was looking at Mom. "A normal life for Chandler or Austin?"

"Well, I meant Chandler, the one on the TV, but Austin, too. I assume he'll be in prison forever, and what he said about his mama. What a monster. As for his life," she said lightly, "I couldn't possibly care less."

I heard Munch's voice again. "I can't breathe." Then the sides of my vision caved in, and I could barely call, "Mama." I don't remember hitting the floor. That's what I'd told him. Day after day. With my actions. Then my words. "I couldn't care less."

Chandler had reported, "Then he said: When I was nine, my mom gave me a hamburger with glass in it, a light bulb. That's the first time I knew. I found a little shard of glass on my plate. Later that year, when I fell off the trampoline, that's when I knocked out my tooth, she wouldn't get it fixed. It was just an opener for her. 'My son, he got brain damaged when he fell off the trampoline. That tooth is the least of my worries. A traumatic brain injury changes a person's whole personality. He has seizures. He could die.' That's what she'd say. I could die.

"I didn't shoot the school because of bullying or jocks versus geeks, or anything like that. Or because of a brain injury, like she'll say. I did it because I have to get away from her.

"Munchhausen, looked it up after I heard Miss Warden say it. Means like a egomaniac who wants all kinds of attention. She's been hurting me to do it. Now she'll get the attention she wants, but I'll be free."

———————

I woke up when it started raining. I listened to the rain, and felt, more than I had in a long time, the sadness of my childhood bedroom. The tap, tap, tap became a steady insistent roll, and I pictured the bloody stains I'd left on the sidewalk washing away. I listened to it until the dawn lit the windows, and I knew that it was too late for Mama to make me take her to mass. Or maybe it was Saturday? I didn't know.

But I knew I was hungry. I wondered if I would have to tell my mom once more how traumatized I was over the shooting or embarrassed over the panties to get her to make me some biscuits and gravy. God, I should buy that stuff. That should go on my grocery list for her instead of steel cut oats, I Can't Believe It's Not Butter and Splenda.

At least I bought good coffee, and Mom had a cup waiting for me at the table, with Edna curled around my place mat, bits of tuna juice still flecked on her whiskers.

"Thanks, Mom," I said, and it seemed, suddenly, like I hadn't seen her for a very long time. "What day is it?" I asked, feeling stupid. "It's Saturday, right?"

"No, Baby, it's Friday," she said, shaking her head, not looking at me at all like I was crazy or stupid, bringing the half and half.

"When was the shooting?"

"Tuesday, and Manny and your friend were here on Wednesday."

"What happened to Thursday?"

"You were sleeping mostly, but you were up some, mostly screaming, and a very nice doctor brought you some medicine."

"My doctor? Dr. Peter?"

"No, isn't he a vet? Why would he come?"

"I don't know. I just didn't know who." I drank my coffee.

"A doctor from the parish. Father called him."

"Did you know he was inside with me?

"Father Nguyen?"

"No," I said.

"Who? Honey, where?"

"Peter. He went back inside with me. To get my kids. I think I should thank him."

"Maybe you'll get to when everything calms down," Mom said, and put a bowl of oatmeal in front of me. Damn.

13

"Starbucks," Manny said when I'd asked him where we were going.

It was the first Starbucks to be built in our little town. "It's not open yet, Little Man," I said.

"You haven't called me that in a long time, sis."

"You haven't acted like it." I looked out the window. I'd naturally climbed into the passenger side when Manny came to get me.

"I know it's not open, still under construction, but that's where Krista said, and she's not the kind of woman you can argue with."

"No," I answered, "she's not the kind of woman *you* can argue with, I do just fine."

"Time to live again, Ellie," he said. "You've been in bed long enough."

"Yeah, I think I got a bedsore." I'd gone right back to bed after the steel cut oats and another pill from the mysterious parish doctor who made house calls. I think it may have been one of Manny's high school friends in a lab coat the way that one pill knocked me out. Even when I woke up screaming, I didn't remember it. Mama said she gave me hot tea. That traitor, trying to make me a Yankee when I wasn't looking.

He pulled into the parking lot between a cement truck and a black Volkswagen Beetle, a new one, with an actual flower in the bud vase. The magnetic sign on the door read: Harmon Veterinary Hospital.

"Crap, Manny. I can't talk to Paula, do you know what I did to her son? I dragged him through the gates of hell. Jesus. Manny, you clown turd, get me out of here. Where's Krista?"

Peter was leaning against the column of the unfinished Starbuck's.

"That's the wrong Dr. Harmon."

"Yeah, that's the kid's dad or something."

"His uncle. He was on the news with me. I carried him off the football field."

"He looks way different," Manny said squinting at him.

"Yeah, he looks pretty normal when he's not being really weird. He was inside with me. He saw all those dead kids." Peter smiled and waved, his hand flapping up and down like he had a puppet on his hand, a puppet that was banging his head to Metallica.

"Get out," Manny prompted.

"Where's Krista? Where does Mama think I am?"

"Krista's not coming. I'm supposed to drop you off here. This is her social planning. I'm picking her up to go to the lake. You are at the church for grief counseling." he smiled.

"Use a condom, but not in my car. I mean don't have sex in my car." I didn't move. "I can't get out."

"Well, too bad, sis, I've got a date." Manny beckoned Peter over to the car.

He opened my door. "Ellie," he said. "I wasn't sure if you would come. I'm glad. I'm glad to see you."

I grabbed on to the forearm he offered stiffly, and pulled myself up. "I'm sore," I said as an observation, mostly to myself, which was good because no one acknowledged that I'd spoken. Manny pulled the door shut from the inside, and Peter raised up his pants leg and showed me his boot.

"Paula told me to wear my boots because you're kind of an Amazon," he said happily.

"Yeah, I'm a freak. I grew up next door to the nuclear waste dump."

"Oh, where's that? Out near Trenton Drive? Do you think it's safe for you to still live there?"

"Number one, that was a joke. There's no nuclear waste dump that I know of. Number two, how do you know the street I grew up on—and where my mother and I do still, in fact, live?" He looked confused, and I knew I had talked too fast, but I just wanted to sit down. "Why are we here?"

"The book said that the first date should just be a meet-for-coffee-date, possibly at Starbuck's, in case the daters actually hate each other, coffee's quick. Date over. But you were supposed to drive your own car. Now, even if we hate each other, I'll have to drive you home, which could possibly cause false expectations on your part if I don't like you, or could provide me the opportunity to take advantage of you if you are the one who dislikes my company."

"This is not a date. And it is not a meet-for-coffee date because there is no coffee here. It's not open." I pointed to the coffee shop.

"I know. Duh. I brought coffee." He went to his car and took out an honest-to-God woven picnic basket and two fold out canvas chairs.

"Listen, Peter," I began, but he threw a hand up.

"I know. You didn't agree to this. You didn't know it was a date. You were tricked, and you are feeling betrayed. Airedale, borzoi, clumber spaniel, Dandie Dinmont."

"No, listen, for gracious sake. My body and my psyche are so bruised I can barely stand up. It's going to be over a hundred degrees today, and it's already sticky and hot. The last thing I want is hot coffee, and the last place I want to have it is at a construction site." I took a breath. "Are you still saying dogs in your head?"

"Ibizan, Japanese chin, kuvasz, lowchen. Yes, but I will stop now."

"Just take me somewhere we can sit down and enjoy air-conditioning."

"We could go to the furniture store," he said.

"Denny's."

"Denny's," he repeated and folded the chairs and juggled the basket into the tiny backseat of his car. He plucked the sunflower out of the bud vase. "The book said not to bring flowers, but since that is plural, I just brought you the one."

The ride to Denny's out on the highway was quiet until I finally said, "Thank you for coming into the school with me, and I'm sorry that you had to. That you had to see that. Do that."

"Me too. I mean, I'm sorry that you had to. And the kids."

"Yeah that was my fault," I started.

"You shot those kids?" he asked.

"No, of course not, I meant I shouldn't have taken them by that room."

"I know what you meant. I can joke too. Not very well, and rarely at the right time, but I can make a joke."

"No, sorry to burst your bubble, but a joke is, by definition, funny."

"Actually, that's not true. Dictionary.com says a joke can be a matter that need not be taken very seriously."

"Please don't make me work hard today," I groaned.

"I'm sorry. You were in shock, and you took the shortest route. Really, there was no way to know there would not be more carnage taking a different path." He parked at the Denny's and dashed around to open my door.

He offered his arm again, and I took it, needing it actually, to unfold myself out of the car. "How's Nathan?" I asked as we walked inside.

"I'm not sure. He's not talking about it, and I'm not very good at evaluating the non-verbal." We took a booth in the corner, the only one available. Peter continued, "So he could be totally unfazed or be ready to start shooting people naked from a bell tower."

Of course, his "shooting people naked from a bell-tower" comment was said just as the waiter came to take our order. I hope he wasn't offended by the reference to the UT shooting. Many people use the phrase, but few people know that it actually refers to a shooting in a real tower on the campus of the University of Texas, but I think the shooter was clothed. I'd have to Google it.

"I'll have biscuits and gravy with sausage. And a Diet Coke," I told the waiter.

"Yeah, me too," Peter said. We'd not even opened the menu. I, of course, had decided on my order while still lying in my childhood bed days ago. "But coffee instead of the Coke."

"Diet Coke," I repeated.

"Got it," the waiter said tartly. I was sure he would spit in my drink, but I'd rather drink saliva and Diet Coke than regular Coke.

"Does the Diet Coke cancel out the gravy calories?"

"You saying I need to watch my caloric intake?" I asked.

"Well, yes. Everyone does, but I'm sure that's not what you meant. I think you meant do I find your body appealing so, again, yes."

"Wow," I said. The waiter returned with my soda and a carafe of coffee. "Can I get a short stack of chocolate chip pancakes too?" I asked him.

"You bet," he answered, writing it on his pad and walking away shaking his head.

"What? No salad with fat free dressing on the side, fatso?"

"Clever," I said. "And brave. So why are we here, Peter?"

"You said you wanted to come here," he reminded me, a concerned look on his face, like I might have amnesia.

"No, I mean on a not-a-coffee date," I clarified.

"Well, the coffee shop was not open, as you so astutely pointed out," he smiled. "I wanted to go on a date with you. Is that confusing?"

"Yeah, actually, a little."

"You sure do say 'yeah' a lot for an English teacher."

"And y'all. I say that too."

The waiter dropped the plates on the table. Too many plates, one for each food, like he thought we were a couple of OCD freaks who could not allow our food to touch. Maybe they know him here, I thought.

I iced the pancakes with butter and poured on the maple pecan syrup, and asked, "Where'd you grow up?" right before I dug in. I hoped he would talk for a while. I was starving. I couldn't remember the last time I'd eaten. Except for tasteless oats, which looked a little too much like desiccated cat rectums for me to enjoy them. And the taste. That kind of ruined them too.

"Yeah, but it's good for the system, if you know what I mean," Peter said, and only then did I realize that I'd spoken the words out loud. The words: desiccated cat rectums.

"I'm sorry, I've been medicated." I swallowed a bite of the short stack. "And traumatized. I didn't mean to say that. Where did you grow up?" I repeated, then asked, "You want some of these pancakes?"

He forked some in and chewed before answering. "I grew up in Vermont. Moved here when I was seventeen and graduated here. Of course, it was different then. More rural. My parents were vets, large animals." He ate another forkful of the pancakes.

"Were? Where are your parents now?"

"They died," he said.

"I'm sorry," I said.

163

"It's okay, I bet you had nothing to do with it. Car wreck." He filled his fork again.

"I said *some* of the pancakes, greedy, back off." I scraped the food off his fork, but he end-ran into the half that was left. "What do you mean here? You graduated here?"

"Not at Denny's. That would it make it difficult to get into vet school. Even at Texas A and M. That was a joke."

"Hmmm," I said, starting on my biscuits and gravy.

"We moved here in 1996, I guess. I finished up my senior year, graduated a Savage in 1997," he said forking a gravy soaked wedge of biscuit into his mouth, and then spitting it into his hand. "God that's awful."

"A Savage," I said.

"Sorry, I don't know how you all eat this stuff."

"Vermont is not the gravy state. What are you going to do with that?" I indicated the blob in his hand with my raised eyebrows.

He plunked it onto his plate, "Let it stay with its friends, I guess."

"So you're a Savage? But not here. Not a Shoemaker High Savage."

"Yeah, Ellie, we graduated the same year. I walked across the same stage and shook the same hands as you did.

Same night." Suddenly the gravy and biscuits in my mouth tasted just like what they were, old grease, weevily flour, and past due milk. And baking powder. Just like Mama used to make.

"Peter. Peter Harmon." I said. The name was not even vaguely familiar, and ours was not a huge school. "I don't. I mean, I can't. I'm sorry, I don't remember."

"It's okay. You probably shouldn't. I was in Mr. Humphrey's class. Like Nate, but we were in the basement then, with only a window unit. God, it was hot."

"You were in the behavior unit?"

"Let's call it protective custody. But, yes, I was there."

"Oh my God, why?"

"Why is Nathan there? Or any of them? Geez, Ellie, what do they teach you in teacher school? But I know what you're asking. I wasn't labeled. I had no diagnosis. I was just a pain in the ass to teachers, students, my family, strangers."

"But why, what did they call you? That's not what I mean." I tried to stuff another mouthful in, but I was just done. "No diagnosis? Just this-kid-is-weird?"

"Not just weird. My family moved here for both of us. Me and Paula. She was given a basically honorary diploma up in Vermont because she was pregnant. Although we are the same age, I was a year behind," he raised his hand to stop my question, and I automatically thought to reinforce his non-verbal interpretive skills.

"Okay, so twins, both seventeen, her with a diploma and a baby on the way, me with an obvious intelligence and a record of starting fires." He took a drink of his black coffee.

"Fires?" I asked thinking of all the serial killers who were first arsonists.

"Yes, fires, but only in the unoccupied backpacks of male students who had earned that rite. And I mean r-i-t-e. I thought of it as cleansing." He drained his cup and reached for the carafe. "For them not for me."

"Holy crap, Peter."

"Hold your sacred feces a minute," he said, "I was actually the valedictorian of your class."

"No," I said slowly, "I was."

"Nope, you made the speech, which was only proper since you'd attended school there your whole academic career, and I was just a Johnny-come-lately-to-the-basement."

"What did it say in your dating book about dethroning your date from the only seat of sovereignty she's ever sat?"

"Oh, I don't think it would be sanctioned, but I'm a rule-breaker, a rebel. And this is a date?"

"Yeah, I think it is," I said. But I wasn't sure why I thought so, but I believe it might have something to do with the way his perfectly shaped bald head held large wide blue-green eyes. And the way I could see the muscles in his arms harden in just the act of pouring coffee, and his guileless smile. And the freckles on the back of his hands. And the perfect arcs that his blond hair made on his forearms, like spidery filaments.

Krista careened out of the copy room right in front of me, a stack of behavior charts under her arm, and her fingers flying across her phone.

"Hey, don't text and drive," I said. "You're not, by any chance, answering the thousands of texts I sent you over the weekend are you?"

"Sorry, and no I'm not, so sorry again," she said, finishing her text. "Ellie," she said, looking at me as if she'd not really noticed I was there before. She hugged me.

"It's fine." She hugged me harder. "You didn't have sex with my brother in my car did you?"

"Of course not. It's much too small, what is he like 7 foot tall?"

"Jesus, he has a Camaro, and I know he's managed that before. Anyway, thanks," I said unlocking the classroom door.

"It looks weird out here, huh?" The school had been closed just a couple of weeks, and they'd managed to paint the walls and replace all the windows that Munch had broken. The halls, though, were still bare of all the banners, posters, and flyers that usually tangled on every vertical surface. "Last winter when Munch threw a chair out the window and into the parking lot onto the hood of Mrs. Grumby's Altima, it took them until spring break to replace the window with safety glass."

"What are we going to do today? How do you do this?"

"I have no idea." I flipped open my lesson plan book. "Social skill for the day is Eye Contact: When, Why, and For How Long. Maybe instead we should do, what? How to cleanse your memory of dead bodies posed before a brain spattered wall?"

"At least it's only a half day," Krista said.

"Yeah, you can do anything you hate for half a day. Even a whole day, my mom constantly reminds me. That's how long she was in labor with me, 24 hours."

"Crap, I forgot. How did your mom take your date? What's his name? Because she almost shat herself when Manny brought me over."

"He took you to my mom's? God, don't forget to invite me to the wedding."

169

"So?"

"Krista, the kids leave at noon for the memorial service, let's process it then. Your date and mine," I smiled in what I hoped was a coy way, but I'd never had a reason to be coy so I couldn't be sure. "Right now, we have about twenty minutes to prepare to address our emotionally disturbed kids who I accidentally led into the aftermath of a slaughter perpetrated against their classmates by one of their own. Any ideas?"

"Yeah, listen."

"Okay, shoot," I said waiting.

"No. I mean we just shut up and listen."

"Let's have them journal first, get their thoughts together. I stopped by Wal-Mart and got this black paper and some gel pens," I said. And, as I had for the past 10 years—or the 28 since I'd started kindergarten, depending on how you count—I forgot my love life and got lost in school.

Brian did not come to school, and I suspected that he would not for a while—if ever again, but Trevor, Jackie, Trixie, Walter (The Whale), Becca and Nathan all arrived on time looking hollow-eyed and tragic. I knew I would have to use their real names. They had to be real people to me in a way that Munch hadn't been.

"Jacky, what happened?" Krista asked as soon as she saw her. I never would have asked, but I was glad that Krista went there.

"I told you Daddy would kill me," she said then smiled, "but it wasn't as bad as I thought." She touched her face, "I probably wouldn't have even needed stitches if I hadn't had that damn barbell in my eyebrow. But lucky number thirteen."

"Thirteen stitches?" I asked, looking.

"Only six here," she pointed. I didn't ask where the other stitches were.

The students and Krista and I were all hunched over our fancy journal paper when it happened.

"Bang, bang, bang," Trevor grunted. "Sorry," he said, not looking up, but I was already on my feet, my key poised for the deadbolt, and Becca was under her desk.

Krista had turned as pale as her desktop. "Do you have a new tic, Trevor?" I asked pointedly. I would never have called attention to his tics under normal circumstances.

"Sorry. It's a pretty bad one. Worse even than the one I had in middle school." Trevor had originally been put into a unit when he developed a tic of yelling out "nigger" when he was in sixth grade. Well, he was put in the unit when he returned to school after being released from the hospital.

"Yeah, pretty unfortunate," I agreed. Becca returned to her desk. Jacky was blowing her nose with a Kleenex from a box of tissue she'd brought with her that morning.

He broke out red across his nose, his nostrils flaring and his chin wrinkling up like a peach pit. Then he was sobbing. "My sister," but he couldn't complete the thought. Trevor had an older sister, a junior. He put his head down.

"Is she okay?" Jacky asked.

"I started in my sleep Tuesday night," he said. "Loud, and I apparently have a remarkable talent for mimicry." He tried to smile, but he put his head down again and sobbed. Poor girl, must have scared her to death.

"Do we need to hug it out?" I asked, and he nodded without lifting his head. When I walked over to the Red Square, they all followed me, and we piled quite inappropriately on top of each other like a litter of puppies and cried and held each other for the next three hours stopping only to blow our noses occasionally, and evacuating the couch for a short period when Nathan farted.

"I sure do love those little lunatics," I said when they had all disappeared into their parents' cars in the carpool lane.

"Are you sure?" Krista asked.

"Yeah, sadly," I answered. "But I think we have a different love life to discuss. Tell me everything," I said, leading us back into the building, past the ISS room, boarded up, and up the stairs. My path with Peter last Tuesday.

"I will not," she answered in a pretense of haughtiness. "But I'll tell you the PG version."

"No, even that will be too much," I reconsidered. "Just tell me that you used a condom," I begged. I tucked the doorstop under the open door. The room smelled like a locker room, or worse. I thought about Krista's adrenaline in the body fluid theory. Inside, I lit a candle, which I kept along with the lighter under lock and key in the snack closet.

"No, of course not, my new boyfriend is a devout Catholic."

"So he took you to mass on Sunday? I didn't see you there," I challenged, trying to channel my mother. I threw her a Mr. Goodbar.

"There was prayer. Kind of," she said, popping it in her mouth.

"Is your convict boyfriend going to make me an only child?"

"Geez. I don't know. I haven't thought that far. I haven't really thought since Wednesday. Tuesday, really. Just feeling."

"I know what you mean," I agreed.

"And tell me about your guy," she said a little reluctantly.

"Well, his Dating for Aspies book told him to take me for coffee, so Manny dropped me off at the Starbuck's." Krista looked guilty. "It's under construction, as you know, so Peter pulled out lawn chairs and a thermos. I swear to God," I said when Krista gave me a skeptical look. "Then we went to Denny's and he spat his food into his hand when it did not please him and dropped it back on his plate. I'm pretty sure he ate it later, though."

Krista was rolling with laughter. I continued, encouraged. "So I was having some pancakes, which is what God created Denny's for, right? And he reaches over and starts eating off my plate."

"No, no he didn't," she shrieked in laughter.

"Then, you're going to love this, he tells me of his unrequited love in high school. He was in the unit with Humpy back in the day! He would have been valedictorian, instead of me, but he was locked in the attic, or basement actually, like the wife in *Jane Eyre*," I said. When I saw her blank look, I corrected my literary allusion, "Like the beast in Beauty and the Beast?"

And we were laughing again. "You invited me to have some of your pancakes," Peter said from the door. "I'm glad you are doing well. I know I'm not good at judging emotions, but it sounds like you're doing okay. I'm glad I could be Ophelia's gravediggers for you," he said, turning. His plastic shoes slapped down the hallway slowly, and then faster with running.

"Shit," I said.

"What the hell? Who's Ophelia? Gravediggers? How inappropriate." Krista said haughtily.

"It's *Hamlet*. It's from Shakespeare."

I5

As I left work, the sole news van not at the memorial service or staked out at the victims' houses, or mine, followed. I drove by Manny's first, thinking that having them harass him for a few days would be gratifying, but Krista's car was already in the driveway, and I didn't want them hounding her so I drove on aimlessly until the driver got bored with me when I prepared to go through the drive through car wash a third time.

Mom had dinner on the table, bless her. Beans and ham with corn bread and fried potatoes, nothing green in sight but the place mat. "I thought y'all got out at noon," she said when I walked in throwing my briefcase on the couch. "Put that in your room," she said, and I obeyed automatically.

"The kids got out at noon," I said returning to the kitchen. "We stayed for some training. Grief training stuff, and awareness training. Did some lesson planning," I sighed. "Tough day, though." I broke a crust off the cornbread.

"You didn't have enough grief training on Saturday? I added sugar for you, just like Jiffy makes."

"Thanks, Mom. Why didn't you tell me that Manny brought a girl here on Saturday?"

"It wasn't a girl, it was your friend. I'd met her before," she said too nonchalantly. "Besides, it's none of your business," she said, dipping the beans into a bowl.

"Bull," I said, "really, why didn't you tell me?" I crumbled the cornbread into my beans.

"He asked me not to," she said. She squirted ketchup all over her potatoes and then unleashed a mound onto her beans.

"Why? And since when do you respect your children's confidentiality?"

"I resent that, missy, I keep my kids' secrets."

"That's only because we don't tell you any of them."

"Oh, I know plenty," she said. "Really, I just didn't think it was an appropriate time to gossip with you being responsible for saving the lives of a couple thousand high school students with your mad kung-fu skills."

"Those aren't your words. Manny said that?"

"Yeah," she said, shrugging.

"Okay, it worked. But Krista's boyfriend is in prison. So Manny maybe needs to acquire some kung-fu skills."

"Couldn't hurt. Maybe I need some so I can kick that slut's butt next time she comes here. Sassy little thing in a bikini that you couldn't catch a guppy in. Nothing to it but skin."

Mom ate her beans, and I had this flash, not insight, not an epiphany, but a premonition. I would be alone, like Mom, having a few beans with my bowl of ketchup like Lenny, rubbing Edna like a dead mouse in my pocket. *We ain't like a lot a guys*, George said in my head. And Lenny answered, *'Cause I've got you and you've got me.*

It is difficult to cry with a mouth full of cornbread, but I was exceptionally motivated. After I sucked a few dry crumbs into my lungs with my heaving sobs, I let the mouthful of cornbread drop into a paper towel, no better than Manny. Or Peter.

"Ellie that's disgusting," she began then remembered herself. "Honey, I'm so sorry. What a hard day for you." She hugged me to her, and I burrowed my face into her neck fat and let myself be led from the table. I had to bend dramatically at the waist to keep my head on her shoulder, but this was the only George I was going to have so I held on.

Of course, everyone knows how *Of Mice and Men* ends, and Mom reported that's what I was screaming when she dropped me on the bed. She tried to give me a pill, she said, but I called her George and refused it.

It was still light out, just barely, when I woke up. For me, Edna always had a chirp and a purr, sounds that belied her size. For strangers, and other threats like squirrels or a wayward moth in the house, she had a yowl that was more befitting a 30 pound cat. She packed a hiss, a spit, and a rapid claw to back it up.

"Edna?" I called her to me, but she wasn't in the room. She'd been staying close to me ever since the reporters had set up camp in my yard, and I'd been awakened that first night several times by the sound of her rumbling growl. Or perhaps by the vibration it sent forth, but now my bed was still. The roar continued, with only short breathing breaks.

I was surprised to find myself still in my school clothes. I normally changed into

179

running clothes as soon as I got home so I would have no excuse not to run, even if I got sucked into a good rerun of The Beverly Hillbillies. All dressed up and you got some place to go, that was my pep talk.

I walked into the living room, "Where's Edna?" I asked Mom, who sat at her table with her endless beads and her Rosary pliers. Every convict on the third coast must have one of Mama's handmade Rosaries. I wondered if Krista's boyfriend had one. I wondered if he was Catholic. Or if she was.

"I put her outside, she was wreaking havoc on my beads," she said. "You feeling any better?"

I looked at her bending the wire into perfect tear drop shapes, hooking each bead to the next with a pair of tear drops. "No, not really," I said. "I'm going to get my cat. Something's up, that's her stranger danger alert."

"Yeah, the news is here. That reporter who saw your underpants was standing beneath the live oak just chattering away on the news."

"Why didn't you tell me?" I growled. Now conflicted. I didn't want to face him or his viewing public, but I had to get my kitty.

"Well, I figured you'd had enough for the day."

I put on Mama's house slippers and went outside. The news van was still parked in front of the house, but no one was in sight. "Edna?" I called, and she stopped her growling for a quick, petite chirp.

"Thank God, this thing's trying to kill me," a familiar voice said. I followed the sound of it, and that of my cat, up into the oak tree where Jeff Blaine, the reporter, was straddling a limb, ball moss in his hair and terror on his face. Edna sat two feet away, in the crook of the tree with her whipping tail hanging down almost as long as the man's legs.

"Edna, honey, you need to come down. You're going to get hurt," I said.

"What about me?" Jeff squeaked.

"Screw you," I said. "I like my cat a lot better."

"That's a cat?" he asked incredulously, his arm extended, his finger pointing, his gold watch dangling. And Edna struck, whap, whap, whap. She was after him for the cleanup, but he drew back farther down the limb. The door to the van slid open. The black-haired lady and the cameraman were there, holed up in the van, but filming just the same.

I did not hear the limb crack, but Edna must have, and it silenced her. She was still. He was still. Edna saw her opportunity and attacked, flinging herself onto him, landing on his back. Then they both came hurtling, screaming down.

From underneath him, you could see paws locked into the flesh of each shoulder, and a still tail hanging between his legs. I kicked him over and picked up my cat. She was quiet and limp, but I could feel her breath.

"You killed my cat, you monster," I said, and I kicked him. I would have assaulted him further, but I had to take care of my cat.

The black haired lady and the cameraman put Jeff in the van and left. The place was without reporters for the first time since the shooting. There was no one there to take me and my cat to the hospital. Great.

"Mama," I screamed as I ran through the door. "Edna's hurt, I'm going to the hospital."

"Aren't you gonna' brush your hair? I don't think Dr. Rimey is open, it's after 9:00."

She was still talking when I slammed the door, running.

Peter opened the door in his boxer shorts. They had Cartman from South Park on them. "I have my cat," I said, holding her out.

"Ellie, what happened?" Instead of inviting me in, he grabbed his keys and pushed past me. I followed him to the clinic. It was dark, and I was glad for the motion activated light even though it blinded me. His Rottweiler, Worf, was having fits, barking and jumping on me, but Edna was limp in my weakened arms, unresponsive.

I babbled the story as we crossed the short lawn and he unlocked the back door to the clinic.

"Has she been alert at all? Have you checked her breathing?" he asked rapidly, but he was lifting her out of my arms, laying her on the table, and checking for himself. I was free, then, to cry. Peter's butt had a speech bubble, "Respect my authority" on it.

183

The clinic was silent against the barking of the dog outside. Three examining tables were set up in a row, tilted like the autopsy tables I'd seen on CSI. There was nowhere to sit.

"I need to sit down," I said, "I'm going to pass out."

Peter did not even look up. I lowered myself to the floor and watched him. He shaved her little arm, and took two vials of blood, and then started an IV. "What's that?" I asked.

"Mannitol injections for any cerebral edema and just fluids right now," he said shortly. "Maybe later we'll administer steroids."

When the phone chirped, I thought it was Edna at first. He answered. "Hey," Peter said, "no, it's just me. Yeah, Ellie Warden's brought her cat in. Craniocerebral trauma. She was squashed by a reporter falling out of a tree. Yes, she's here." He was silent for a minute. "So what was I supposed to do, Paula?" He waited. "No, I don't need you here. I can handle it." Silence. "No. Paula? Paula? Dammit."

"She's going to die?" I asked.

"Paula? No, she just got a call from the security company. I forgot to disarm the alarm," he waved his hand toward the back door.

"No, my cat. Is she going to die?"

Narcissistic Praise-Junkies

"Probably," he said.

"How do you know?" I demanded.

"I don't know, for sure, but probably."

"Is she hurting?"

"I gave her something for the pain." He looked at my nose, and tried to meet my eyes, but couldn't. "Your second opinion will be here soon."

I started to lift her off the table.

"Don't touch her," he said.

"Why, am I going to hurt her? Make her deader?"

"There's something I've got to tell you."

"No, something I've got to tell you. I'm sorry for what you overheard at the school. It was a tough day, and we were just trying to relieve the pressure. Usually we have kids to make fun of in the afternoon, but they'd been just little lumps of grief. I know I exaggerated stuff, like you eating off my plate, and outright lied about other stuff like unrequited love, but I—I'm just kind of mean, Peter," I said.

"Ellie, I'm afraid of cats," he said, almost looking at my eyes. "I mean, really terrified of cats."

"You're a vet," I said stupidly, finally picking up Edna, as though he might hurt her.

"Yeah, I do all the cat surgeries, dentals, neutering or whatever. They're asleep."

"How can you afraid of little kitty cats?" I looked down at my little Eddie, she opened her eyes a little, just a crack, and chirped. I lowered my face into her mane and sobbed.

Peter walked around the table and wrapped his arms around me and my cat, hooking his chin over my shoulder to pull himself up a little. I sighed and leaned back into him, quieting. "We need to keep her warm, put her in a warming crate," but she was plenty warm, wrapped up by both of us. "Cats are too much like people, you just don't know what they're thinking, except that they're probably thinking about themselves, and how they can best make others serve them as quickly as possible."

"Narcissistic Praise-Junkies," I said.

"Exactly," he said, and kissed me, right below my ear. It was soft and perfect, and totally natural.

"That's how I see people. I'm more like a dog," he said, totally serious. "Exactly like a dog, I have one emotion at a time. I'm happy or I'm sad, or I'm scared, and I'll tell you. Obsessive maybe, like Worf is about chasing a ball. And I have no shame. I just do what

186

feels natural, and when people cringe, I just think about Worf, lifting his leg, licking himself, or passing gas. He's just doing his thing."

"I have a book in my classroom, *All Cats have Asperger's Syndrome*. I love that book. *All dogs have ADHD*, that's another one."

"Yeah, Paula got that book for Nathan, that's when I thought up my dog and cat theory."

"And when you began to fear cats?"

"Oh, no, I've always feared cats. My parents had the whole population of the ark at our farm," he stepped away from me, and without thinking, I stepped back into him. It felt so good. He held my arms to hold me still, and stepped firmly away, and turned me around to face him, and wrapped me and Edna up again, his head resting on my shoulder, his mouth speaking into Eddie's fur. "I was an annoying little gasbag, you know how we are," I nodded. I knew in two senses of the word. "But I always knew when the dog was going to nip me, the goat was preparing to ram me, or the donkey kick me. Even the cow warned me before pinning me to a rail fence and crushing my ulna." He pulled back to show me his scarred arm.

"But I could never read a cat. Our perfectly docile cat went for my jugular," he pulled his stethoscope off and pointed at what looked more like a snake bite scar or a vampire mark. I leaned in and kissed his throat carefully. "See, people are just as unpredictable. I stand too close, and you lunge for my throat."

When the backdoor opened, Peter sprang back from me like I'd really tried to bite him. She walked in efficiently and scrubbed her hands. "Give her to me," Paula said.

"No," I said. "Peter's got this, we're going to put her in a warm thingy."

"I'm sorry, Ellie," but her face did not show sympathy, only anger and tension, "but Peter can't handle this. I fear you both have overestimated him." She took Edna from me, her hands infinitely more gentle than her words. She cradled her easily, a woman who has held an infant. She lifted the cat's eyelid, lowered her face to Edna's. "See, Peter? She's dead. You couldn't even tell the cat was dead? I'm sorry, Ms. Warden." She closed the flow from the IV, and removed the tube.

"Me too. I'm sorry," I took Edna from her. "I'll take my dead cat and go."

"Ellie," Paula said, but I heard nothing from Peter. I just kept going.

I got it. I left her kid in a time of the highest stress of his life, embarrassed her twin brother on now-international television, and then laughed at him, I'm sure he'd told her that. She was probably glad my cat was dead.

But she followed me out into the yard. She touched my arm, and I turned toward her, but I couldn't hear her over Worf's barking. She tried to usher me back inside, but I refused, shaking my head and walking away. Paula went ahead of me to my car and let herself into the passenger seat. I tried to sit down in the driver's seat but Edna wouldn't fit between me and the steering wheel. She took her from me, and I tried to hold on for a moment, but I saw no reason to play tug-of-war with a dead cat. Paula held her and stroked her head. "Poor baby," she said.

"I know. She was such a good cat. Twelve years. Slept beside her every night. It's like losing a really hairy compliant spouse."

"I wouldn't know about that. Never bothered to have one so I never had one to lose."

"My mama would have said that was pretty smart. And I would have agreed with her until very recently."

She sighed. "Losing a pet is like losing a family member, a son, a brother. You brought my family out of that building. Thank you."

"I don't overestimate your brother. You overestimate me. Don't thank me, that's the last thing you should do after what I led them through to get out. Besides, there was no danger when we left."

"And why was that?"

"The police had the shooter," I said.

"How?"

"They just took him."

"After you found him, disarmed him, called for help, and turned him over to the authorities—after extracting a confession."

"Yes, and before I quite literally dragged your son through a murder scene, humiliated both myself and your brother by association on a news story that is being shown and subtitled in at least 57 countries." I rolled down the window. It was hot, and I was intensely aware of Paula holding my dead cat.

"But I have more to thank you for," she said.

"How's that?" I reached over and rubbed Edna's ear tufts.

"My brother's disability often distorts his reality. I told him that you had asked if he was single; you know, during the Manifestation Determination hearing, and I had to repeat several times that you were not serious." She rolled her eyes, and shook her head as though the

190

persuasion had been exhausting. "Then a couple of nights later you both carried him and walked with your arm around him, which is more physical intimacy than he's experienced in his entire life probably."

She looked at me, "I know that he seems pathetic to you, and you could have just refused the date, even though he insisted you two had a rapport at the crime scene. At first I was glad that you'd gone out with him, even though I was scared too—how he'd behave, how miserable you would be, but he came home so happy. Bubbling over. I don't think he'd ever had a date before. Well, I know he hadn't.

"He asked Nathan what kind of present he could get you. They went out and bought school supplies. Dry erase markers; Nathan explained how you had little funerals for the ones that'd all dried out."

"Yeah, now I'll have another funeral."

"And a funeral for Peter's little fantasy love. And for that, I thank you." She sounded like Comedy Central's Tosh.0, but I wouldn't admit that I watched that show. At least not to someone I would have to look in the eyes again.

"Wow. I'm so sorry. I didn't mean to."

"No. I mean it. I had to listen to Peter talk about you for all of our senior year, well his senior year and my year of 'lying in' as they used to say, and then last year when you started transition to high school with Nathan, I was stupid enough to say, 'Hey, remember Ellie Warden?' and there we were again back in high school." She petted my dead cat. "I'm glad you did what you did. It was very smart."

"What do you mean? What did I do?" I asked. Lead him through dead bodies? I wondered. No, he came into the building himself. Embarrass him on television? No, again that was his choice.

"Really? Come on, Ellie. He told me everything. You and that Ms. Parker laughing at him. Imitating him? He's had a lifetime of that. If you'd tried to let him down easy, he wouldn't have understood—but that kind of humiliation he gets."

I grabbed my cat out of her lap. I slammed the door and draped Edna across my shoulders, ran back across the boarding lawn losing Mama's slippers, slipping in some semi-fresh, crisp on the outside, wet on the inside dog poop, and banged on the clinic's back door.

Peter opened the door, obviously fearful, pale. I kissed him, dramatically, wrapping my arms around him and running my fingers over his bald head so

Paula gaping through the car window and now running, escaping from the car, would see that it was me. Me stroking his arms, holding his head to mine.

When she reached us, she grabbed my arm, pulling me away from her brother. "What are you doing?" she asked him, then me, "What are you doing?"

"I'm thirty-two years old," he said "And that was my first kiss, and it was from a woman with a dead cat on her head and dog poop on her foot."

17

Peter replaced his phone to his head, "I'm on the phone." Paula lifted the cat off my shoulders and took her to a room that looked like an x-ray alcove.

"We'll call a service tomorrow. You'll have your cat's ashes returned to you in a lovely box. I'm going home." She squeezed my arm before she left, but she did not meet my eyes or even look at Peter.

"Yes, that's what I said," he said into the phone. "A dead cat on her head. That's why I called. Do you have any idea how long I've been on hold? Well, yes, long enough for my first kiss, but I call 911 and I get put on hold?" Peter waited in silence for a second. "Yeah, I said it wasn't an emergency, but only because it's not life or death—someone's already dead." He listened. "That what I thought." He hung up.

"They're on their way, finally," he said, looking at my nose. "You did, um. You did that thing," he pointed to his lips. "But—did my sister make you?"

"Yeah, kind of." His face fell. "She made me realize that I couldn't wait to kiss you, and she had help, a kid I once called Munch. I'll tell you all of it. Soon." He raised his eyes a fraction. A trick, look at my lower eyelids. Count the blinks. I'd taught Nathan that. Waiting and counting can look like listening. "If we are kissing, I'll close my eyes. No eye contact." But I barely got the words out before he was there with me. Reenacting the passionate scene from the doorway.

I put my hand to his face, not to stop him or push him away, but to feel his face, and let my fingers stroke his cheek, soft and slow, set a pace. "If you are going to explain to the officers that my cat was murdered, you need to look like a doctor."

"I'll put on some scrubs."

"You got a lab coat?" I asked, looking at his South Park boxers, Cartman looking a little more aggressively authoritative. I didn't think scrubs would hide that tent.

"Oh, yeah, right. Good idea."

When the officers arrived, Peter answered the door in a lab coat with a stethoscope around his neck, but bare underneath down to Cartman's distended face.

The police officers were relieved that they didn't have another actual murder on their hands. I was pleased to get a restraining order against the reporters. And I could see that Peter was happy when I told the officer that in spite of his heroic efforts, my boyfriend could not save my cat.

It was after midnight when the police left. "What a night."

"Yeah, what a night," Peter grinned.

"What happens now?"

"Let's fall in love," he suggested.

"I don't think we're allowed to," I said. "But I'll get my mom to sign a permission slip, if you get your sister to sign one."

"Can I have a kiss for luck?" And I obliged. "I know why I need a permission slip, but why do you? Most moms would be frantic to find their old maid daughter a prospect."

"I'm not an old maid," I protested. "In my mother's eyes, I'm a—well, I'm her. She doesn't want me to make the same mistake she did."

"What happened?"

"Can we sit down? I'm exhausted."

Peter sat right down leaning against the mysterious cupboards in the surgery room, and I tucked around him so my head could fit into his shoulder.

"Well, here's the story, as I remember it and what I remember mom telling me. Consider, though, that Daddy died when I was six, so a certain amount of skepticism is reasonable.

"So I was born about ten months after my parents' wedding, and while I can infer the actions that led to the conception, I cannot even imagine the emotions, or I didn't think I could. My parents loved each other so much; it was obvious to me even as a very young child that they adored one another. My mom didn't work, and when it was time for Daddy to come home, she would put on her make-up and a nice dress, and I would set the table, or try to.

"Then from the back door, he'd start singing, 'Here comes the sun, doo doo doo doo. Here comes the sun, and I say, it's alright.' And she'd rush back there singing, 'Here comes the sun king, here's comes the sun king, everybody's laughing, everybody's happy.' Then they would kiss and we would have dinner, and everything was beautiful."

"That sounds great," Peter said. "What great memories."

"Yes, good times. And I woke up every morning to one of them singing 'I'm up on top of the world, looking down on creation,' but you know, neither one of them could sing worth a

damn. Then, something went wrong. I
don't know what. I can't imagine.
Daddy got angry and Mama got quiet,
but I heard them fighting at night. Mom
refused to have sex with my dad, as she
reported to me after his death and as I
heard him scream at her during my
formative years. But, at some point,
Daddy raped Mama, and she got
pregnant with Manny.

"The day after the rape, Daddy went
to mow the lawn and, overwrought with
guilt or rage or whatever, he had a
meltdown on the front lawn. It was
horrible, the whole neighborhood saw it.
It was funny to me after a while, but after
too long, I was able to put the timeline
together, and realize what had set him
off.

"He went out and bought a John
Deere riding lawn mower. Not quite a
tractor, but a monster. He parked it in
the shed. And never once mowed the
lawn with it. By the time he died, you
almost couldn't see the house from the
overgrown weeds.

"He had this coffee cup, it said
'Nothing runs like a Deere' and he drank
his coffee out of that cup every morning.
After the John Deere came home, he
would pour his coffee, go out and survey
the land while drinking that coffee. And
then go into the shed, sit in the seat and

start up his tractor, and masturbate, ejaculating into his cup, then he'd take it in for Mama to wash.

"Mama had morning sickness, though. And he probably knew it too. She went out to the shed to tell him. But he was dead. Carbon monoxide poisoning. Never knew about Manny, officially.

"I think Mama might have raised me thinking of the vocations, but she just couldn't turn loose of me," I finished, snuggling into him so he wouldn't think of turning loose of me.

"Yeah, my parents had a similar plan, but as a youngster I would go into the mad rocking, raging tantrums, and my dad would say, 'Oh, yes, there's the leader of your flock, Mary Margaret, what a fine priest,'" Peter laughed, and the vibration echoed through me.

"You're Catholic?" I asked. "What parish?"

"Oh, I go to mass over at the nursing home, and then take Worf around to visit the patients. Then we meet in the activity room and make Rosaries for the incarcerated."

———————

Mom was waiting up for me, and by "waiting up" I mean she was asleep in her recliner with her head on her beading table. When she raised up to greet me, she had three Rosary beads embedded in her fat cheek.

"How is she?"

"She died, Mom," I said.

"Oh, honey, I'm so sorry."

"I know. I'm still in shock. I just can't believe it."

Mama pulled the beads off her cheek and placed them back in her tray. "You poor thing," she said. "What are you going to do?"

"I haven't decided yet. I think I need something to take my mind off of it."

"Get another kitty?"

"No, I think I'm going to fall in love."

"Well, that ought to distract you. Nothing like having your heart mangled by some idiot man to make you forget about having your heart mangled by the death of your cat," Mama said, suddenly awake.

"And the death of six students, one teacher, and the loss of one kid to the loony bin and one to prison forever," I added.

"Yeah, falling in love is just the thing," she stood up and pulled her housedress out of her butt crack. "I'm going to bed."

When I was in fourth grade, I came home for the first time talking about a boyfriend, and although Mama says she never saw the movie "Carrie," she managed an almost perfect reenactment of the crucifix in the closet scene. She dragged me to confession, right then. Face to face in the office of Father Viera. I said the words that I'd practiced with mom, not the Act of Contrition, but Mama's words. Boy crazy, lustful, disobedient, and lecherous.

I could not, however, get forks to fly at my mother's head. Father Viera did reinforce that I was too young for such behavior, and I did not consider boyfriends again until the old priest was dead, but the timing was purely coincidental. I think.

Soon after I turned sixteen, I asked Mom if I could start dating. She told me I was welcome to, but there would have to be some changes. For one, I would have to sell my car because she would not allow me access to a "No Tell Motel" on wheels. Also, there would be no more choosing my own clothes. She wouldn't allow me to advertise myself. My food was restricted because when I inevitably got knocked up, I'd need to have a healthy and lean body. It went on and on.

I decided that it wasn't worth the trade, and as long as I was under my mother's roof, I could abide by her no dating rules, but I just never left home. I couldn't afford it in college, and by then Mama had lost the ability to drive, she said, and couldn't survive without me.

Despite that, during my senior year in college, I seriously considered becoming a nun. I even ordered a catalog of realistic nun dolls so I could determine which habit I liked best. As I was thumbing through the pages, though, the thought, unbidden, came to me, "Not very realistic. These nuns are all young and pretty and largely blonde, instead of old and foreign, and ranging from homely to grotesquely misshapen."

The real deal-sealer, though, was that I had Edna by then, and I couldn't stand to be separated from her.

"Maybe I should become a nun," I said to Mom as she turned in her bedroom door for the last word. Maybe now, twelve years after I'd abandoned the idea, now that Edna was dead.

"You're too old. They'd never believe you're a virgin. They won't take women after 30 unless it's some weird fringe-mission thing."

"How do you know that?" I asked.

"I have the internet, Ellie," she said. "You don't think I considered the vocations?"

"You didn't have the internet when you were under thirty," I said. "So you mean you considered the vocations for me."

I have been created in her image, but she is not God.

"My boyfriend and I will be going to the Pecan Street Festival on Saturday, and then we'll have dinner. Would you like for us to pick you up on the way to the restaurant, or will you be cooking?"

"I'll cook," she said, slowly.

"For five. Manny and Krista are coming too."

18

My cell phone rang on the way to my classroom, and I was ashamed that I immediately thought of Peter and was disappointed to see Krista's number. "Hey," I said, balancing the phone on my shoulder, unlocking the door.

"Ell, I'm going to be late. Manny's car won't start, again, so I'm going to pick him up, and he's going to keep my car today."

"What? A lover's spat? Why aren't you waking up at his house?" I joked.

"I'd already come home," she laughed. "See you soon."

"No, wait. You and Manny and me and Peter are going to have dinner at Mom's on Saturday night. Tell Manny."

"What if we have other plans?"

"Really?" I asked. "You're going to miss the chance to see me with Peter? Ask Manny if he's willing to give up that chance."

"Okay, what time?"

"6:00. And as long as you're going to be late, stop and get me a large coffee. I had a long night."

"Hmm, that sounds interesting."

"Not really. Edna died."

"No, Ellie! No. I'll bring donuts too."

I set down my briefcase and booted up the computer, then there was a knock at the door. Timid.

I looked out the window. Jacky. I swung the door open, "Hey, pretty, how's my girl?" I asked.

"Good, Miss Warden," she said. "Sick," she amended.

"I've heard that's a good sign. Women who have no morning sickness are more at risk of miscarriage. Anyway, that's what I've heard."

"You ever been pregnant, Miss Warden?"

I looked at her surprised. "No, baby, I've never even been married." I laughed, remembering that one could put this cart before this particular horse. I wanted to apologize, but decided I couldn't.

"Why, Miss?" she asked. "Why didn't you ever get married?"

"I'm not dead yet," I said; she looked embarrassed. "I was scared. There are very few decisions that one can make that one cannot undo. Even a tattoo, you can laser that off, but marriage is forever, that's the way I was raised. Raised Catholic. You marry here, you marry once, and you're married forever, eternally."

"No one you wanted to be with forever?"

"Not so far," I said. I was not yet ready to say, "til now." But I did say, "But I'm still researching the topic." I smiled.

Jacky touched her belly. "Here's something you can't undo. Something I couldn't undo, but I know people do. My Mama was Catholic. I don't think I would know that. Daddy never talks about her, but I remember the funeral."

"Jacky, is that—I mean, Jacky. Never mind." If she hadn't shared who the father was, it was just not my business. "You know that we are here for you no matter what. You know that, right?"

"Yeah, Miss Warden, I know," she said, just as the first bell rang.

Krista came in at the beginning of check-in. "Give me some good news!" I was saying in my most forced happy voice.

The students looked at me, unresponsive. I hadn't even tried to get good news since the shooting, but I thought it was time to get back into our routine. "Here's a good thing! Ms. Parker brought me some coffee!" I exclaimed. "Good work. Who else has some good news?"

No one answered. Becca began to cry. I relented, "I know, it's still a little early for good news," I agreed. "I have some good news," I tried for a smile, but tears began slipping down my face. "My little kitty has gone to play in cat heaven where there are plenty of cicadas to catch, and the only food that's served is tuna steak. She must be thrilled," I said. "But I will miss her very much," I finished.

"I've got some good news," Trixie finally admitted. "I saw my dad this weekend, finally, and he didn't even mention my, um...decision. Not even my gender. Didn't call me 'son' or 'Jason' or 'faggot.'" Trix smiled. "He just said he was glad I was safe."

"Great, Trixie," I said, "I'm glad you're safe too. Glad you were safe at school and you are safe at home."

"I saw on the news that Austin's pleading guilty. So there won't be a trial. I was scared about being in court."

"Yeah, I was too, Becca," I responded. I wanted to erase the specter of Munch so I moved on. "Who else has some good news?"

"I had a doctor's appointment Friday," Jacky said.

"What?" Trix said, lifting her fist to her mouth.

"Not that kind of doctor. An Ob/Gyn. A pregnancy doctor. Someone who delivers babies," Jacky said. "I heard the heartbeat, and it won't be too long before I can see it on an ultrasound. Tell if it's a boy or a girl soon."

"How?" Nathan asked.

"The ultrasound sends sound waves and the way the sound echoes back allows a picture to be formed. The doctor can see all of the baby to make sure that he or she is growing properly. After a while, they look at the genitals," I explained. "If they see a penis, then it's a boy."

"They can't tell that, though, can they?" Nathan asked.

"Well, yeah, it may look kind of like a thundercloud on the screen, but the doctors can tell."

"No, I mean, Trixie has a penis, right?" He didn't stop for an answer. "So that's not definitive."

"I'm not sure that this is relevant, Nathan," I said.

There was silence. Krista and I looked at each other, but the kids all looked at their shoes. "So in looking at the ultrasound, the doctors can tell whether the baby will have the body of a male or female," Krista compromised.

"And since the psyche almost one hundred percent of the time corresponds, the doctor can make an educated guess whether the child is a boy or a girl," I said with a sigh.

"I've got a good thing," Nathan said. We all looked at him and waited. Nathan was not a real optimistic person, and he did not have a lot to share during the good news. "My uncle, who is just like me," he began. "He's got a girlfriend."

"Really," Trevor challenged. "Just like you? And he got a girlfriend? Like a mail order bride?"

"The blow-up kind," Walter answered.

"Huh? No, I mean, he's got a date and stuff," Nathan said, confused.

"That's great, Nathan," I said. "I know you are very close to your uncle. I know that his being happy makes you happy too."

———————

The students were already trained to follow the procedures that I'd established during the first week of school. When I had a full classroom of thirty students, I couldn't count on their knowing to sharpen a pencil, find some paper, and open their literature before starting the warm-up until October.

Before the tardy bell had rung, though, my kids were working on their proofreading exercise. All four of them little angels. Trix, Nathan, Becca, and Trevor had adjusted without a hitch to combining their English I and English II classes. Freshman and sophomore English were survey courses, so I had them reading the same literature anyway.

"So does he finally get to the bazaar?" Nathan asked, eager to return to our abandoned "Araby."

"Did you finish your proofreading?" I prompted.

"No, I'm protesting. I think the assignment is unfair," he said.

"Really? I give you an altered newspaper article to revise every day. What's wrong with today?"

"It's about Dub Bush. He had his own language, any of this could have been said."

"I may agree with your politics, but I do not agree with your unlogical argument." He cringed at my intentional error, and I smiled. "Do the work, so you are not a child left behind." He smiled and was already marking the errors before I finished.

"I've finished," Becca said. "So can you tell me if he gets to the bazaar?" We'd left off just as the possibly drunk uncle returned.

"Of course he gets to the bazaar. If he hadn't why would the story be called 'Araby'?" I asked. The kids took this as an invitation to ditch their proofreading, and they opened their literature books. I sighed. I'd lost the heart for Araby. In fact, that's why I chose the Bush story; I thought I could drag it out long enough to skip the literature altogether.

"Alright, guys," I started and Trixie cleared her throat with a very fake, ahem. "Alright, guys and gals," I corrected. "What do you think that this young man will find at the bazaar? What is your prediction?"

"Well, obviously, he's going to get a present for his girlfriend," Trevor said.

"And then what?" I asked.

"He'll give it to her, and she'll love him, and they'll live happily ever after," Trix said.

"Okay, can you find some evidence in the text for that?"

"No, we haven't read it yet," Nathan said.

"But you can analyze what you've read and determine whether or not the author would take the story that direction. Does it seem like Joyce is ready for a happily ever after?" I asked.

All of the kids nodded their heads, "Duh, miss, his life is so depressing. He has to, like, find the meaning," Becca said.

"What if the meaning is there is no meaning?"

"That's a bunch of shit, then. Like that stupid Arab on the beach story you made us read?" Trevor said.

"Watch your language, Trevor," I said.

"It was a tic," he retorted.

"It was not, but no, not like Camus's *The Stranger*," I said, but I wasn't sure if it was true. I was suddenly very ashamed of the literature I'd stuck them with. I took a deep breath and made a mental note to go to confession. "James Joyce does set up a very bleak world for his narrator, except for this one bright spot. Naturally, the author will allow his character to bask in that little ray of sunshine."

"It's just like Cinderella, then, but for a boy this time," Trixie said.

"Yeah," I agreed. "Let me read the end to you. It's pretty short. Y'all want to settle into some bean bags?" I asked, and they all ran to the reading corner like kindergartners. I thought maybe I didn't need to go to confession after all. This lie was going to be okay. I folded myself up onto the floor with them and began my story, pretending to read from Joyce's.

In my story, the stalls were still closing, except for one. This one was run by a wise old woman who seemed to know that our narrator would come. She sells him a lovely bracelet for much less than either would have expected because she can read on his face his earnestness. As can Mangan's sister, who accepts the gift with dewy eyes, the bracelet itself a lesser gift compared to his devotion.

"Gazing into her eyes, through the darkness, I saw myself as a creature driven and devoid of vanity. Her eyes burned into mine, and we kissed." I finished, closing the book.

"That's it?" Becca asked.

"But what happens?" Trixie asked.

I sighed dramatically, "Haven't I taught you anything about literature? You have to infer. Obviously, when he looks into her eye 'through the darkness' it represents the bright spot in his life. Her eyes, in return, burning, shows her returned love."

"That doesn't seem very realistic," Nathan said. "I bet he turns out like his drunk uncle, and she gets fat and has too many kids, and she yells all the time."

"Just shut up and have a good time, Nathan," Krista said.

"Yes, ma'am. When you put it that way, how could I refuse? But I bet that bracelet he gave the girl wasn't real silver anyway, and when her arm turns green, she's going to be pissed."

"That'll do, Nathan. Let's get our stuff ready for third period. Becca, you okay walking alone?" I felt weird asking her since I'd been sending her out to walk the halls with a lunatic murderer for the past few weeks.

"Yeah, Miss Warden. I'm good."

"Anybody else need an escort?" I asked, but the bell rang, and no one stayed back clinging to my skirts, figuratively of course. I would never wear a dress or skirt to school again.

"You know, Miss Warden," Krista said, "that's not the way I remember 'Araby' at all."

"Yes, but you are getting old, and you've been sleep deprived lately, and with your substance abuse during your earlier years, I don't think your memory is very reliable."

"What are you reading to them next? The love story of Othello and Desdemona, where no one dies at the end?"

"Why, yes, Miss Parker, I'm glad you've taken time to study your syllabus."

"You wanna' tell me about Edna?"

"Not really. She died. I took her to Peter's clinic, but it was too late."

"I'm so sorry, Ellie," Krista said sincerely, but I could tell that there was another thought behind her words.

"And, yes, then I made out with Peter over the corpse of my cat," I answered her unspoken question.

"Oh my God," she squealed, sounding kind of like Trixie. "And it was?" she prompted.

Without warning I started to cry. It was like my emotions had developed a case of hiccups. "I don't know, Krista. It was perfect. It was, I don't know. It just was."

Krista sat down on the sofa and I sat at the other end, my legs triangled up so I could rest my head on them. I wiped my eyes on the knees of my jeans and tried again, "It was like crossing the finish line after running a marathon," I said. "While being chased by a bear," I added.

"Through the streets of Dublin," Krista said shaking her head, and we were both able to laugh. "Sorry about your cat," she said and hugged me over my knees, leaving her head there. I scratched behind her ear.

"I'll be okay," I said.

"You always are," she answered.

"You act like you've known me for years, instead of just weeks."

"It's been the longest weeks of my life. No offense intended."

"I'm offensive enough without taking on yours," I answered.

I thought that canasta was a poor replacement for high school football, but Mama and Peter seemed perfectly happy to play, especially since we were having a rare cold night. Even in December, the hill country had been stubbornly warm, until tonight.

While Mom racked up the points at Peter's naïve expense, she rubbed her feet along Worf's appreciative back. She laid down her fourth red three and smiled.

"I hope you are not doing anything you will have to go to confession for," Peter said.

"Oh, I'll probably be stopping by anyway," she said casually. "Guess I'll probably be seeing you there," she added, acting as if ensuring he were present for Christmas Eve mass were not a milestone.

"Yeah, he's still saying Hail Marys for stealing your daughter away. When, oh when, will he attain forgiveness?" I asked from the couch where I was watching Big Brother alone.

Peter's transition from Hamster-Neutering Daughter Thief to canasta partner hadn't happened over night, but it hadn't taken as long as I'd thought. If I'd known Mom would be won over so easily, just over three months, I might have started bringing home men a long time ago, and have three or four marriages under my belt by now. No, that was the thing. That's why she accepted him. Because he was the real thing.

At that first dinner, Mom had been eager to hear all the details I'd held back from the shooting, and Peter, lacking the same emotional speed bumps, had divulged all. After describing to her precisely the color and consistency of brains on the wall at twenty minutes past impact, she had finally sat down instead of standing over him. Vilifying the black haired producer who had, obviously, broken the elastic in my underpants as she manhandled me, eager to get the scoop, earned him an actual offer of a beverage.

By the time he'd wrapped up with his remembrance of my valedictory speech, she was cutting him a second slice of store-bought pie. There'd only been a slight hindrance when Mom had suggested that the shooter should be sent to the electric chair. A lively discussion on the equity of capital punishment had ensued, during which Krista and I finished the second bottle of wine. By the time Mom had suggested that Texas should fry them all and let God sort them out, and Peter had challenged her to admit that "them" God would sort out would be mostly darker than her own skin tone, and they'd agreed that "all of us" are guilty of something, and we all rely on the benevolence of God's mercy, available at the local church (as long as it started with "Saint"), he was in.

Neither of them was compromising when they toasted to the mandatory neutering as a condition of parole, and I suggested that we relocate to Gun Barrel City, Texas. Of course, Gun Barrel City, Texas is difficult to say when you are slurping down your fifth glass of wine. They didn't listen, however, because Peter was diagramming the actual neutering surgical procedure on Mom's neglected calendar whiteboard, using Worf periodically as a model.

The next week, when Peter drew a three circle Venn diagram to take notes as Mom delineated the varying rules of high school, college, and professional football, she was ready to date him herself. They left the Savages' win over Killeen shaking pom-poms that Peter had made for the two of them, while Krista, Manny and I followed behind bewildered but buoyant.

Krista's progression had been more problematic. She still wasn't allowed in the house without Mom's sniping under her breath. Peter had suggested once while he and Mom battled the grill flames which was compulsory with the grilling of hamburgers, that perhaps it was because Krista wasn't Catholic. Mom had replied, loud over the roar of the fire extinguisher, that it was because she was a whore with a husband in jail.

"We broke up, and anyway, he was not my husband," she had exclaimed, forgetting to ignore their impropriety.

"I'm sure he is," Mom replied without saying anything about the marriage of the flesh, but Peter had been happy to clarify it for everyone. Manny and Krista had gone together to pick up the pizza, and when they came back he had scratches on his face, and her eyes were puffy. But she stayed. In fact, stayed with Manny, moving into his apartment during the first week of December. She wasn't allowed to answer the phone or the door yet, though.

"How long before she's beaten you soundly enough that you'll surrender?" I asked as Big Brother ended.

"We just started another game," Peter said.

"Well, Sisyphus, lose more quickly this time, I'm getting bored."

Mama threw in her hand, "I've had enough victory for tonight. I'll let you have him," she told me.

"Good, I have a great Vietnam movie from Netflix," I said cheerily, a sure way to get mom to go to her own room. I was sure that Peter and I were both developing a sick fetish due to making out endlessly to the sound of machine guns, screaming napalmed men, and falling mortars. I ordered movies based on the level of violence and the length, and we weren't above watching the director's cut.

"I don't know how y'all watch that stuff," Mom said, swallowing her night time pills.

"It's historical. Our personal history," I declared, "both our fathers fought in that war." She wouldn't argue with that.

"Alright then, I'll see y'all tomorrow," she said and kissed both our cheeks and gave Worf's ears a vigorous rub. "You watch these two," she told the dog.

As soon as her bedroom door had closed, Peter grabbed the movie and headed for the DVD player, and I went to brush my teeth. I no longer gave myself stern talks in the mirror, but it had taken a couple of months. I'd started with, "Don't act like you are thirteen. Good grief, you are a grown woman." And that had progressed to, "Stop acting like a tramp," and then, "How many times do you have to be told no?"

In private, Peter and I were like Siamese twins, joined at the lips, but the only thing that happened below the neck, in conjunction, was hand-holding. I'd thought it was being in my mother's house, a matter of respect, but when I'd suggested we go for a walk, or a drive, or a hotel room, he'd only said, "I'd prefer not to." So I renamed his penis "Bartleby" from the original "Cartman," but it was apparent to me, always, that it was not Bartleby that preferred not to, but Peter.

When I came back from the bathroom, minty clean, Peter had the movie on, but was standing, waiting for me. "We need to talk," he said, almost meeting my eyes. The look on his face and the feeling in my body, head to toe, was reminiscent of our first night together.

I was filled with dread.

"Ellie," he took my hands and we sat down together on the couch. "I'm not a proud man. That's good for me, because I've been humbled my whole life. When I was in sixth grade, I actually had to have my stomach pumped after the boys in P.E. made me eat urinal cakes. They do not taste like cake," he said.

"And when I had the audacity to attend the freshman formal, alone," he continued, "I was pantsed during my first ever dance with a real girl besides my sister. And 'pantsed' actually means de-pantsed," he explained. "My first day in college, I pulled the fire alarm in a frenzied panic when my roommate and his friends were smoking marijuana in our room. I thought the dorm was on fire. They actually broke the bong over my head," he tilted his head down, parted his hair and showed me the scar.

"Zounds, Pete, is this some sort of new verbal foreplay? I'm getting all worked up," I joked.

He took a deep breath. "Eloise, Ell, I can't have another milestone in my life corrupted by my stupidity. No. Not stupidity, but my inability to accurately assess the situation." He hugged me hard and kissed me softly in the indention behind my earlobe. I felt his breath on my neck, but I felt it everywhere. Just like the first night, the first kiss. It was a momentous kiss. Not my lips, not my cheek under the watchful eye of my mother.

"Are you breaking up with me?" I asked, intending a joke, but tears formed in my eyes.

"Ellie, you may be as clueless as I am," he said. He bunched my hands together and kissed at them, the noise resounding, magnified. "Tomorrow, after we go to mass with your family. When we drink spiked hot cocoa, listen to A Very Elvis Christmas, and open presents, you are going to open a little package with an obscenely large diamond ring. And when I humble myself, on my knee, before your family and ask you to be my wife, I don't want to—"

"Yes," I said into his lips, as I kissed him. "Yes," into his neck. "Yes," into the indention behind his ear. "Yes," looking into his eyes in the missed second that I was able to hold them.

I did the same thing twenty-four hours later with Manny and Krista and Mama, and even Worf, watching us happily.

It certainly was not a shotgun wedding, but I don't think I could have been in a bigger hurry to marry Peter if I'd actually been in labor. We'd decided to get married over spring break. A small wedding. On that time line it would have to be.

We were doing it all ourselves to keep Mama from worrying too much about what she should have been paying for, in her mind. Of course, she couldn't afford anything except the rice confetti so we were keeping it beyond simple.

The wedding would take place in the small chapel at St. Matthew's where Mom and I, and Manny until he was eighteen, attended mass every morning at 6:00, Monday through Friday. It would hold only about 50 people, and we would have the use of the activity room for the reception afterward, only because Mom's Rosary club had been strong-armed into relinquishing it for their Saturday afternoon meeting.

225

The one thing that we were really working hard at was procuring the "centerpieces" for the reception tables. We had decided to find vintage toys for each table. Toys we had played with as children. Perhaps it was silly or even arrogant, but we wanted people to recognize two things: we were old and we were still innocent children. I would be thirty-three and Peter thirty-two when we got married, but we were just like kids, just as excited. Additionally, Peter was terrified that if there was dancing, someone would force him to dance. He was convinced that he would never recover from that humiliation. He also knew that no one would want to dance if they had cool vintage toys to play with.

So on weekends, Peter and I—or Krista and I when Peter had a vet emergency—trolled through flea markets and garage sales all over central Texas looking for the right toys. So far we'd found an Etch-A-Sketch, a Magical Musical Thing, a Weeble's Haunted House, a Lite Brite, Simon, a Speak and Spell, Spirograph, Pianosaurus, and an Atari console. We were looking specifically for a Battleship game, a couple of View Masters, Baby Chrissy and anything else that caught our fancy.

Peter especially liked the outdoor flea markets because he could bring Worf. I was less of a fan because of the February wind, but we did find some amazing stuff. There was a lengthy debate in front of a vendor who had a Milky the Marvelous Milking Cow; although the set was complete with even the tablets to make the water white, neither Peter nor I had had one as a child so we weren't sure it was appropriate.

I made Peter buy it, but he wrote it down in his notebook as an "unacceptable compromise." There was then a debate about whether that was an oxymoron. When I finally had to give in and use the blue phone-booth sized Port-a-Potty, I left Peter with an Action Jackson set with 20 changes of adventure clothes, a Hungry Hungry Hippos game, and an internal debate about the accuracy of the moniker Port-a-Potty. "You can't really carry it," he said.

"You need to be thinking of who to add to the guest list so we have people to play with all of these toys," I said, hanging the last bag on his arm, catching my ridiculous engagement ring in the plastic and ripping it open. When we were out in certain environments, I turned the set inside my palm, paranoid that someone would wrench it from my hand.

"I think we need a Ouija Board," Peter said, kneeling to pick up the View Master circles.

"Are you trying to kill my mother?" I asked. "Don't answer that, I have to pee."

The inside of the potty was sprinkled thoroughly, as though some man had danced the Hokey Pokey while urinating, but I'd waited in line for fifteen minutes, and I was sure that none of the other toilets were more pristine. It was a difficult maneuver to hover in a Port-a-Potty, much harder than in a bathroom stall where you usually have walls to brace against. My six foot plus frame further complicated matters. But I was a determined hoverer, having been taught basically along with the original potty-training that you never ever sit on a strange toilet. You poise yourself over the toilet, suspending just the necessary part over the germ-laden, and in this case urine-spritzed, latrine.

I couldn't allow my jeans to bunch around my feet either, as I normally would because there was a puddle there. By the time I'd dropped my drawers and bunched up my panties and jeans in my right hand clutched between my knees and prepared to brace myself with my left hand against the back wall, my bladder was about to explode. Ready to unleash, so to speak, I placed my hand on the wall, my ring settling into a soft goo. I lurched forward but, unable to stop my overtaxed bladder, I quickly realized that a mysterious goo would have been preferable to the soaking that my underpants and jeans got. I sat down heavily on the dirty seat, finishing.

"Crap," I said, "well, yeah, I guess it could have been worse." My right hand was dripping urine. My pants were soaked, my left hand had goo residue, which seemed to be, mercifully, just gum. And my butt was wet from the previous users. I stood up and began to cry. "Dammit, dammit, dammit, dammit," I cried, and kicked the door, which flew open, knocking Peter down since he'd leaned up against the door to protect my privacy. But now there I was, naked from my waist to the wet pants around my ankles. I could feel the urine now soaking into my socks. There was a line for the stall, and I wondered if they would be terribly eager to come in after me.

Peter stood up and saw me naked in the doorway, and closed his eyes, "Ellie, pull up your pants!" he said, as though this hadn't occurred to me.

"I can't," I said even as I reached down and pulled the wet jeans up to where they belonged. "Okay," I said, then he opened his eyes, and hugged me, pulling me out of the door of the dirty little booth. "I'm sorry," I cried.

"It's hard to believe that you've lost your panties in public twice now in six months, when that doesn't usually happen to anyone at all, unless they are receiving some remuneration for it, or you're pantsed at your freshman formal," Peter commented. I continued to sob.

"This is not a problem," he assured me, but he wasn't the one with itchy thighs and a growing stench.

"Even my socks are wet," I sniffled, hanging my head.

"It's okay, you had to wait in line a long time. Everyone has accidents some time. Usually it's running a car into a light pole or something worse. So this is not that bad, see?"

He had his hand on my lower back, a dry spot, and hurried me through the crowd to the parking lot. We were at least an hour from home. I sobbed some more, snot dripping freely, my hands were not clean enough to wipe my face. Worf managed to walk mostly backward with his nose stuck to my crotch.

230

At Peter's car, he opened a large blue case. "We will have you fixed up in no time," he said smiling.

"What is that?" I asked.

"My road kill kit," he said in a way that made me mentally add the "duh" that was implied. Peter would naturally pick up any injured dog—or injured and firmly unconscious cat—he ran across, or over.

Inside, he had a set of clean scrubs folded neatly in a gallon size Zip-Loc. Underneath that, a gallon of purified water, gauze, a large muslin sheet, and various bottles of medicine. A syringe and some ampoules were in a smaller case. Cold packs and hot packs.

"Okay, let's get you fixed up." He ripped the muslin into strips and dampened them with water from the jug. "Wash," he commanded.

"Here?"

"Oh, wait," he took a blue plastic sheet and threw it over the open back door to create a little privacy. Inside, I stripped off my dirty clothes, and Peter put them in a plastic bag. I noticed he had gloves on. I wondered if he would wear gloves when he changed diapers some day. My diapers when I got old? And hopefully babies' diapers soon. Very very soon.

Bathed, naked and barefoot, I asked, "Okay, what's next, Doctor? I don't guess you've got any underpants in there."

"Here, put on this scrubs top, it will hang down far enough."

"Far enough for what?" I asked, but I did it and handed him my shirt. "My shirt isn't even dirty."

"You've got to match. Scrubs are a set. Okay, I'm coming in," he said dramatically. His face was flaming red. "Panties!" he said holding up the roll of gauze. "Just no more going to the bathroom. On yourself or anywhere else." He wrapped the gauze around my waist and between my legs, around my hips and back again, all with his eyes tightly shut.

"I'm glad you didn't become a gynecologist," I said.

"Or a urologist," he quipped. He swiped a long strip of tape across my right hip, and I pulled up my scrub pants, then sat down on the back seat. Peter pulled down the curtain, poured some water on another muslin strip and washed my feet before slipping them into his extra pair of Crocs.

"I love you," he said.

"You must. But I can't imagine why," I said.

"Ready to go home? We can get to the vigil mass if we hurry. You can sleep in tomorrow morning."

He took one more strip of muslin and washed my face with it, meeting my eyes. A gift.

Instead of our planned lunch out, we picked up Mama's favorite fried chicken and went home. I was so humiliated by my accident that I hadn't even considered what Mom would say about my change of clothes. And she didn't waste any time. "Eloise Warden, what in the name of Jesus happened to your own clothes?" she demanded, invoking the name of Jesus so I couldn't lie.

"It was my fault, Mrs. Warden," Peter said with no hesitation. "I loved the funnel cake so much that I had a second. One bad bump, and I vomited all over Ellie."

"Oh, you poor baby, I'll get some Pepto," she said, rushing off. He went into the kitchen to swallow the two spoonfuls while I threw my ammoniac clothes in the washer.

"I keep a spare set of scrubs in the car just in case I get dirty picking up an injured or stray animal," he said, trying not to make a face.

"I'm going to go change. Y'all start on the chicken, and don't pull all the skin off my pieces, Mama, I know your dirty tricks."

I jumped in the shower, grabbing the toothbrush Mom used to clean the grout

233

so I could coax the grime out of my ring. I had thought the ring was ridiculous. Ostentatious. A three carat ring in a cushion setting, so it sat up a half inch from my hand, would be joined by another carat wedding band. Peter had explained, though, why the ring was necessary.

About a year ago, a young couple had come in to Peter's office with their Rottweiler puppy, Dork. The dog had apparently swallowed wifey's ring. They wanted Peter to open up the dog and fetch the ring out, like a plumber pulling the jewelry out of a drain. Peter told them that the surgery would be very expensive and that a free option would be wait until the ring passed. "How much to put the dog to sleep," the man asked, angry. Peter told him it would be $100. "Okay, let's do that, and I'll go in and get the ring myself."

"So you are willing to, with no veterinary training, perform a post-mortem on a dog so you can get the ring out 12 hours sooner?"

The woman began to cry. "We're getting married in the morning."

"I'll remove the ring," Peter had told them, "but I'm keeping the dog." The couple had agreed. Peter had believed that people who would name their dog Dork in the first place, and then hack up its body to find a diamond chip ring, were not worthy to have a dog. And when Dork came out of the anesthetic, Peter explained this to him. "He wrinkled up his little forehead like he was really listening to me, and he looked just like Worf. So that's what I named him," he had explained.

"But why the huge ring?" I'd asked.

"It won't be as easy to swallow," Peter said.

21

I fervently hoped that no one would recognize my entrance song as Enya. It said only, "Fairytale," in the order of the mass. Someday I would reflect that it was amazing that on my wedding day, that was my biggest worry. Not whether I was ready or had found the right man, but only that my song was tacky.

"Do you wish Daddy were here to walk you down the aisle?" Manny asked.

"No, I never even thought of it. The day is perfect just as it is."

"You going to start crying and acting like an idiot?"

"Nope. I'm going to leave that to Mama. Besides, Krista had me chew up a couple of Xanax a couple of hours ago," I said.

"You might sleep through the honeymoon," Paula said giving Krista, my other bridesmaid, a stern look.

"There's no chance of that," I said.

The music rose, and the ushers swung the doors wide. Everyone stood, Mama smeared at her mascara, Father Nguyen smiled broadly, and Peter had his back to me. "Turn around, turn around," I heard Paula say quietly between clenched teeth, but the walk was short, and I was there in seconds to touch his elbow and turn him to me. He looked up at me, not into my eyes, but at my hair, my veil, then down to my flowers and then my lips. "I love you," I mouthed, and I got his eyes for just a second.

"You look pretty," Nathan said loudly, breathily, beside Peter, and the assembly giggled.

"No, you do," Peter said, and turned to give them a stern look.

"Thank you," I said to both of them.

"In the name of the Father and of the Son and of the Holy Spirit," Father Nguyen began. Peter's hands were shaking so badly, he whacked himself in the head while trying to make the sign of the cross. Nervous. About the ceremony, or the marriage?

By the time we got to, "I confess to Almighty God, and to you my brothers and sisters, that I have sinned through my own fault," our voices were cracking so badly we sounded like Trevor. The rest of the liturgy was simple, just the mass that I knew as well as my own name, and the vows we had rehearsed. Then *Whither thou goest there also shall I go*, and *The greatest of these is love*, and *For richer, for poorer, in sickness and in health, all the days of our life.*

We had decided to have Paula and Nathan, Manny and Mama come to the altar for the lighting of the wedding candle, which was serendipitous since neither of us could have managed the aiming and the lighting with our quaking hands.

I was tempted to take a long drink of the sacramental wine, but decided I could probably make it through the rest of the liturgy without the fortification.

Peter and I held on to each other and stumbled back up the aisle to Israel Kamakowiwo'ole's "Wonderful World" like a couple of drunk sailors, laughing and crying.

It had been a tough negotiation, especially with Paula, to determine what traditions would be omitted to accommodate for Peter's disability. "If you are able to get married, you are not too disabled to kiss your wife." But there was no *You may kiss the bride.*

I negotiated directly with Paula for the whole garter thing, "I fully intend to lift up my skirts for my husband," I told her, "but I don't intend for the first time I do it to be with an audience." We did link arms to drink champagne, and delicately and respectfully feed each other cake, but when I sucked Peter's finger to get the last of the icing, he turned as red as his rose boutonniere. And he had to sit for a while.

We loved seeing our friends and family running through the reception hall pulling a Digger the Dog, or a Popcorn Lawnmower. Manny started Weeble bowling, not a sanctioned activity, and had to be restricted to the Lego table. Mom tried both the Pogo Stick and the Lemon Twist after a couple of glasses of wine. Mr. Humphrey let Paula show him how to milk the Marvelous Cow, "I haven't done this in years," she kept exclaiming.

Despite constant complaining, Nathan played Pong for over an hour, until Father Nguyen made him give it up to play Q-Bert. The cacophony of the Magical Musical Thing and the Pianosaurus, the Simon, and the splat splat splat of Q-Bert, was a little overwhelming to both Nathan and Peter, and they played some basketball in the parking lot for a very short while. Paula gave them some earplugs, a stern lecture, and led them back inside. They played Rock 'em Sock 'em Robots, screaming their challenges and trash talking at each other because of their earplugs.

I'd really thought that the reception would be fun. We'd planned for it to be, but it may have been the most miserable thousand hours of my life. "You sank my battleship" and "My Easy-Bake cake is done!" continuously made me want to then suggest that they go home and enjoy the rest of their evenings. Too many toys. Finally, I paid Nathan fifty bucks to go around jerking toys away from guests and putting them in the toy box. With his snotty hands, it did not take too long for people to decide that it was time to go home and bathe in Germ-X.

I'd attended weddings, many weddings, and it had never occurred to me how eager the bride and groom would be to get rid of everyone. I believed, though, that we were especially libidinous, having waited. It was a party, a celebration for these two people, and they wanted nothing more than for the party to turn stale and prosaic. At least there was no dancing.

"At our kids' weddings," Peter whispered to me, "let's serve Hamburger Helper and no alcohol."

"That will save us some money," I agreed.

"And my sons some frustration," he said.

"Sons? And daughters, I assure you," I said, sighing.

"Let's have a tournament," my distant cousin cried to the stragglers, gathering up the four board games: Mousetrap, Battleship, Don't Spill the Beans, and Life. I'd never liked her.

"Nathan must have missed the board games," I said.

"I think she was hoarding them," he said.

"Let's get out of here, husband, and don't you dare say you'd prefer not to."

"Oh, I do, wife." He reached his hand under my pure white satin dress, hooked his finger in my garter, rubbing my thigh with the back of his hand. "I prefer to."

"To what?" I teased.

He pulled the garter down my leg, off my ankle, and threw it behind his back where it landed on Manny's head, "I'm taking my wife out of here," he yelled.

"You have your games to play, and we have ours," I said loudly.

Peter tried to pick me up, but he was standing on my dress, and it tore as he lifted me, though not too badly because he only lifted me inches off the ground before we both tumbled to the floor. Even like that, having his body next to mine was an invigorating torment, and I stole a kiss. "Let's go."

No one had time to bring out the rice to shower us as we left in our undecorated car. Two more traditions failed.

The Driskill Hotel, where we would spend one night before leaving for our real honeymoon, was a twenty minute drive. On the way, we played the Nonsense Game to keep our minds in order. "Name five things you shouldn't stick up your nose," he started.

"Crap. Okay, that's one. Cocaine, two. Your friend's finger, a lit firecracker—three and four. Um, your penis."

"Five. That's five," he agreed, reddening and shifting in his seat.

"Yep, I said penis. Name five businesses that could never be successful in Dime Box, Texas."

"Combination abortion clinic and tattoo removal, a Wheatgrass Juice bar, an ear-candling service, and a Wiccan bookstore."

"That's four."

"No, abortion clinic, tattoo removal," he held up two fingers.

"Name five things you are looking forward to tonight," I said.

"You just had your turn."

"Okay, then I'll tell you," and I leaned close to his ear.

He threw me his Blackberry. "Call the hotel and tell them we are on our way, and Dr. and Mrs. Harmon expect check-in to be quick and easy."

"That's how I like my men, quick and easy," I said, dialing.

Our valet had to pick up the keys off the sidewalk, where they finally landed after Peter thrust them at his hands. The twenty dollars I urged on him caught a gust of wind, and I didn't see where it went, and did not have the inclination to chase it in my still unsoiled, though slightly torn, wedding dress. Maybe he'll just steal something from the car. Some of our wedding presents were in there, so maybe he could get an engraved soup tureen or something nice and useless like that.

"Dr. and Mrs. Harmon," the receptionist greeted us, ringing the bell. A man who looked like a Tim Conway creation instantly appeared with a luggage trolley and loaded our things. I felt reddened, not embarrassed, but raw with my emotions and pulsing with thoughts I was sure could be read even by Peter.

"We don't need help. We got it," I tried to manhandle the trolley away from the old man, but he was stronger than he looked. He minced along as if his shoes were tied together, pushing the cart with three wayward wheels.

"That's not the way we do things at the Driskill," he admonished, his prune-like face wrinkling into further distortions.

"How old are you, mister?" I asked abrasively, "because I'm guessing, generously, that you are not yet 65, which is our combined age. I would also wager, again generously, that you have probably had sex at least once in your life. So here's the thing. Together," I swung my finger maniacally between me and Peter, "we are sixty five plus, and we have not yet had sex in our lifetimes. And today is our wedding day, and if you don't give us that trolley and point us to our room, we are going to 'consummate' right here, and I'm guessing that it won't be pretty to watch." I gave him a second to evaluate how little we looked like porn stars.

He handed Peter the envelope with the key, and gave me the luggage. "Top floor. Turn left," he said. "Have fun," he chuckled. Peter took off toward the elevator, and the trolley and I squeaked along behind him. In the elevator, I heard him.

"Malinois, otter hound, puli, no Q, Rhodesian ridgeback, saluki," he said quietly.

"Peter, why the dog parade?"

"Why? I'm nervous. Oh my God, you're not nervous?"

I hadn't thought about it. "Well, no, I don't think so."

"Tibetan spaniel, no U, vizsla, whippet," he continued.

"Are you going to be okay?" I asked.

He held up a finger, wait. "Xoloitzcuintli, Yorkshire terrier, no Z," he breathed, and the elevator dinged and the doors opened. "I'm going to be great."

"I know you are," I said and grabbed his earlobe between my teeth.

"Akita, basenji, Chinese crested, Dalmatian," he said.

"Left," I said, leading the way.

The room was beautiful, gleaming dark wood floors were scattered with thick rich colored rugs, an antique grand piano, tables laden with fruits, a wine and cheese and breads tray and an arrangement of flowers as tall as Peter filled the room while still leaving room to play rugby if the notion took us. Marble columns and sparkling chandeliers delineated a hallway ending in a gold drape that marked the passage to the bedroom.

By the time I'd thrown our bags off the trolley, and booted it back into the hallway, Peter was sitting on the edge of the loveseat with his trembling hands grasping his knees, his back straight, his face pale in contrast to his flaming ears.

This was football field Peter, and I was the line rushing at him. "Hey, Husband, I'm going to go change into something more comfortable," I said, and he became more wan. What saint does one pray to in this situation? The Apostle Paul? Why shall I marry and still burn?

Our bags were stuffed and heavy, packed for Scotland, but I dragged them two at a time into the lush bedroom. I couldn't lift them onto the bed, and I didn't have time. Peter's clothes were folded into tight squares, sorted by color.

In the third layer I found what I was looking for, his scrubs. Dr. P. Harmon stitched on the breast. Two pairs: one in light blue and one in khaki. I put on the blue ones, leaving my wedding dress in a heap half covering the luggage.

In the sitting room, Peter was still sitting stiffly. "Let's get you out of that monkey suit," I suggested, holding up his scrubs. His shoulders lowered a half inch, and he looked toward the upper part of my face. Was this the same man who'd pulled my garter embroidered with our names from underneath my dress in a room full of our family and friends?

"Thanks, Ellie," he said, but his hands were shaking and, while the jacket came off easily enough, the cuff-links almost caused a break-down.

"Let me," I said.

"No, I—I don't think I'm ready."

"Okay. Then, what? Your shoes? Does that sound okay?"

He sat down on the loveseat, and put his right foot on his knee, but he couldn't manage the laces. When I pulled the string, he jumped.

"Afghan hound, border collie, collie," I began.

"No, you can't put the two collies together. That's cheating," he said, and I lifted off his right shoe.

"Yeah, um, then, let's see," I pulled the laces and lifted off his left shoe. "Corgi," I said.

"Cardigan Welsh Corgi," he said. I lifted his left hand, kissed his new ring and unhooked the cuff-link at his wrist.

"Doberman pinscher," I freed the other cuff. "English...something," I said.

"Foxhound," he said, and closed his eyes, and stretched his neck. I pulled his tie loose easily.

"Great Dane!" I said as an exclamation. And softer, "Harrier," as I undid the first buttons of his shirt and touched his chest for the first time, catching my fingers in his chest hair. Under my hand, he heaved a breath, opened his eyes, and smiled.

"I have music," he said. There was a Bose CD player tucked in a corner.

"Can you manage that, or do you need help?"

"No, I can," he stood up and went to the bedroom, looking quickly behind him at the door.

"Don't worry, I'll stay right here." And try to think of a dog that begins with I. Probably an Italian something. I reached under my scrubs top and unhooked my bra, pulling it out Flashdance style and stuffing it under a large brocade sofa pillow large enough for Worf to use as a dog bed.

He came back in the room with a pink jewel case. I recognized Trixie's handwriting, our names hooked together in a loopy heart. "Nathan?" I asked.

"Yeah. He called it B sides that don't suck."

"Great," I opened the wine. White wine, not champagne, the unpredictable cork would freak Peter out, I had told them. They must have thought that Peter was my retarded Pekingese. There's a dog for P; I'd have to remember that.

249

The music started, and I heard, "Now put your hands up/up in the club/we can't break up/we're doing our own little thing/you decided to dip/now we're gonna' trip," not in Beyonce's sexy voice, but in Jacky and Trixie's giggly karaoke.

I helped them out, changing the words to fit the occasion. "I liked it so I put a ring on it," I sang, jumping clumsily onto the piano bench then to the cocktail table to the love seat and to Peter's lap. He was too surprised to recoil, and he finally laughed.

Elvis Presley's Hound Dog inspired Peter to do an awkward strip-tease, safely concealed behind the sofa. He then inconspicuously put on his scrubs while I shouted the words to "Into the Groove."

We were weakened by our laughter when we finished our disco version of "I Will Survive" and I lay down on the thick Persian rug. He laid his head on my chest, a little wet with the sweat that had run down from between and under my freed breasts. I tried to catch my breath, and I was conscious of his listening to my thumping heart.

"Remember how you got pantsed at your last dance?" I asked and gave a forgotten cartoon laugh.

Soon, I was breathing again and I simply spoke the words along with Righteous Brothers. "I've hungered for your touch. A long, lonely time. And time goes by so slowly." I felt the tears run down from my eyes onto my neck, into my hair. "I need your love. God speed your love to me."

My husband pulled the waist tie loose from my scrubs, and turned his face into my belly. "I'm sweaty, don't," I protested, but I didn't mean it.

"You're salty," he said, his lips moving against the skin of my heaving-again belly. "And sweet."

"You know that's not true," I said, but I felt myself lifting myself to his mouth. His tongue flicked into my navel.

"Sweet," he said, and he lifted his eyes toward mine, and I felt a tiny splash on my stomach. We were both going to cry about it. "Sweet love." He raised himself to his knees. Kneeling beside me, his face streaked and flushed, he looked like a saint, lit from within, kneeling at the altar of my body.

I arrived in the bedroom with only the scrubs shirt and my lacy underwear, the bottoms having been abandoned along the way. I tried to do two things. Breathe and look at his face but not his eyes.

251

Three: wait. I could wait. I would have to wait.

He lifted his shirt over his head and returned his eyes, I imagined, to the pulse in my neck, where his eyes would normally rest, both of us barefoot. I wanted to keep my eyes on his face, but I couldn't. Of course, I'd felt his chest, rested my head or my hand there, but his exposed chest, firm and proud, defined, was new.

I ran my hand across him, feeling his warm flesh, the texture of his hair, pushing my fingers into the hardness of the muscles, moving my finger to his biceps, more familiar, and squeezing the strength there. I heard "I Love U in Me," a B side from Prince, but was smart enough to keep quiet. I closed my eyes.

"Wife," Peter said, resting his right hand curved along the top of my left breast. "My wife." I lifted my top off my head, but left my eyes closed; I couldn't have stood it if he looked away. I stood there, as vulnerable as a person could be, naked but for the lace, the breath, the blood, the body. "One Bread, One Body, One Lord of All," our communion song.

His lips felt cool. Like an overdue rain. And our bodies were together, breath, blood, and body. Hot, except for the

drink of his mouth on mine. Then on my
neck, and breast and belly.

23

We never made it to Scotland, but we took turns reading aloud to each other from the travel books we'd bought so no one would ever know that we'd never left Austin. We drove our car to the airport, parked in long-term parking, and took a taxi to a somewhat cheaper hotel where we spent most of our time in bed. We ordered a lot of pizza and Chinese food.

Sure it would have been nice to explore another country, but we considered that we had a whole new world to discover in each other. Peter suggested we tell people that we had such a great time in Scotland we were going to return for our fifth anniversary.

After our two week cloister, I thought it would be liberating to be outside, but almost as soon as I thought, "It'll be good to be back to real life," I realized that real life would include going back to the NP unit after Krista and a substitute had been holding down the fort for a week. Even if things had gone well for them, the kids would act out once I returned to recoup the attention they'd not had from me for two weeks, the week of spring break and the week of my honeymoon.

I could also expect a certain amount of behavior from my mother. We'd hired Peter's former caretaker, Nannette, to be Mama's caretaker. Although the duties would be much different, I imagine that the frustration level would be similar. Peter taught her to play canasta, and she could drive, so Mom might turn out to be pretty happy.

It's funny that I hadn't considered that Nannette would be inheriting my irritation, and I would be getting hers. Peter was an askhole, a thing I didn't know existed when I was just a teacher. In my early years of teaching, I said there were no stupid questions. Later, I decided that there were a lot of inquisitive idiots.

Peter, though, asked at least a thousand questions before breakfast was over, and life was pretty uncomplicated in a hotel room with food delivered, and nothing to be done except watch television, read books, have sex, and discuss the future.

But Peter managed to create an inquisition out of every topic. He had lived his life like a pinball, being bounced around, running into people's expectations and bouncing off until he collided with their disapproval. He'd learned, therefore, to ask lots of questions to keep from being surprised by people's boundaries. The first night we'd spent together at the Driskill, it had begun.

To be fair, it had always been present, but we'd not spent so much time together that it had been overwhelming. "So do you like that side of the bed? Is that where you always sleep? Do you want me to shave now or is in the morning okay? Do you squeeze the toothpaste tube from the bottom or the middle? Do you want your toothbrush on the right or the left? Does it matter if they face each other? I always shower in the morning, but I guess I should shower at night, right? If we'll be having sex, don't you think that would be better? When do you shower? I hope we'll have enough hot water if you bathe at night. What size is your water heater? Did you and your mom both shower at night? Did you run out of hot water? Once I had to bathe Worf and then take a shower and there was plenty of hot water then, but Worf doesn't like a lot of hot water; do you like a lot of hot water?"

I tried really hard to redirect him to the things that I liked doing: watching television, reading books, having sex, and discussing the future.

So many plans needed to be made. Plans we'd not considered before the wedding; the first had been whether or not I would continue to work. No, we decided. Peter had suggested that at my age, I needed to start producing babies pretty quickly, and that we were in a unique position to have me stay home and raise them. "Especially if they're like me," Peter had said. Or had Down Syndrome, which was possible too at my age, he pointed out, but I would continue to work up until I actually had a baby. I didn't want to be in the situation of quitting my job, and then not getting pregnant, giving myself countless unfilled hours to ruminate about sperm motility and basal body temperature spikes.

And should we stay at the clinic house, so close? Under Paula's thumb? Or move out to a place with more room and privacy? We'd decided that we were happy to be so near Peter's work, but I wondered if he would continue to think so once he got bored of coming home for a sandwich and sex. At least that was his fantasy, once I was home to provide the sandwich and the sex instead of being at school. Of course then, there'd be babies, and his coming home at lunch would give me leave for a nap.

The biggest question, the one that I introduced into conversation the most, was how soon I could have a kitty.

"You have Scratch, the clinic kitty," Peter had whined.

"I miss Edna," I cried.

"There won't be another Edna," he countered. And by that he meant both that no cat would be the same as my beloved Edna, and that he would not allow me to *buy* a Maine coon when there were shelter kitties being euthanized each day, justifiable homicide. He took my mom's approach of kill them all and let God sort them out; great for cats, unacceptable for human criminals.

I could go to the clinic every afternoon to play with the boarded and sick cats, but I wanted a kitty that I was bonded to. One that would flip its belly to me for rubs and loves. Peter flat refused to consider sharing his house with a feline menace. I asked him to consider psychotherapy, hypnosis, electroshock therapy, and ceasing to be a damned crybaby as solutions for his neurosis. "Your prejudice against cats is that they're too much like people, but you've learned to accept people being close to you," I said on the last morning of our honeymoon as he lay still on top of me, tired and happy.

"You could learn to accept one little kitty, couldn't you, Honey?"

"Ellie, please. Stop badgering me. Once we have children, you will stop obsessing over having a pet," he argued.

"So when I get pregnant, you'll be over Worf? He can just go live with Mama?"

"No, obviously, Worf is a dog. Man's best friend. He's a part of our family."

"A kitty would be too," I whined.

"Listen, Ellie, before we even shared our first kiss, I told you how I feel about cats. I assumed it would be a deal-breaker for you so I wanted to let you know. You've made your decision now. Right?" Arguing with Peter was almost impossible. Or it would be impossible for most people. Like kicking a defenseless bunny. On Easter. With children watching.

He argued without fire, without a commitment to win. With Peter, an argument was just a negotiation over the correct interpretation of facts. "Couldn't you let me have a kitty, and then write it down in your notebook as an unacceptable compromise?" I asked as a final effort, but I knew the answer, and

I was already extracting myself to go cry in the shower.

"I love you, Ellie," he said, grabbing my hand as I slid out of bed.

"I know. I love you too," I said. "I've gotta' get myself one of those notebooks." I was down to my last set of clothes. I pulled out a pair of jeans, and a sexless t-shirt, my travel-over-the-ocean-back-to-reality outfit. Peter had supervised my packing, and as a result, every pair of pants had a pair of panties and a pair of socks in its front pockets. In my last set of clothes, was also my iPhone. I took the charger out of the pocket of the suitcase to charge it while I showered.

Two people, living in such a small space for a week, can create a lot of mess and disorder. And I thought I'd cleaned off a nice space for my phone, before I put it down right in a smear of shaving cream. It buzzed at me, and the battery icon lit up red, just a sliver. Totally dead, and I hadn't thought about charging it even once over the last two weeks. He may not let me have a kitty, but he was certainly entertaining.

I tied my hair up in a tight bun before stepping into the shower. My hair took several hours to dry, and going home with wet hair after a supposed ten hour overnight flight would be problematic.

My shower was perfunctory; I had a lot of packing to do, and we were expected back at home in just a couple of hours.

Even when we were really a part of civilization, my phone never rang. In fact, it rang so rarely that I always connected the sound of the ringtone to that awful call on the day of the shooting. It was Krista. I looked at the time. I wasn't sure we should be on the ground yet so I let the call go to voicemail, and listened to it while brushing my teeth.

"Ell, hey, it's me. Welcome home! We've missed you so much. Great news. Jacky had her baby last night. Wild times. You'll never believe it. Call me."

Wow. Jacky had her baby. I counted on my fingers. This was the end of March, so when? About June? July?

"Honey, is it okay if we make a stop on the way home?" I asked, opening the door a crack. Not there. Probably down in the gym, running on the treadmill. So I'd take that as a yes.

The curtains were drawn over the nursery window, and I wondered if they ever used that window so you could look

261

at the babies like zoo animals. They'd had it when Manny was born. But times had changed: kidnapping, birthing suites, lactation coaches.

"Ellie!" Krista squealed, and I turned, just as she launched herself into me. "You got my message."

"Nope, we just thought we'd stop at the maternity ward on the way home. Along with the kosher deli, the rubberband factory, and the used tire store. Fancy meeting you here," I said, hugging her the whole time. "How's Jacky?"

"Good, and the baby. Tiny thing, just over five pounds, she was about four weeks early."

"So it's a girl?"

"Huh? No, Jacky was early," she said, distracted. "Have you had coffee?"

"No, we're pooped. I'm just going to see Jacks and the baby and go home."

"Her room's down that way. 318, but—well, be nice. And you just be quiet," she said to Peter. "No, Peter, you need to go with me to the cafeteria. Help me carry the coffee. I don't trust you." Krista grabbed his arm, and led him assertively down the hall.

The doors all had cut-out storks holding either pink or blue bundles. Except for Jacky's. Jacky's door had a yellow bundle, and the stork's speech bubble announced, "It's a baby! Welcome, Dali/Dolly!"

It was quiet and dim in the room, and Jacky, looking softer and even docile without her make-up and jewelry, slept with the tiniest little infant tucked in at her breast. A lavender cap had slid down, encroaching onto the pink face, delicate blue veins webbed its cheek. Gently, I lifted the cap to see the wispy, translucent eyelashes and wispy down of the forehead.

"Miss Warden," Jacky said, groggily. "No, I mean, Missus. Um."

"Harmon. How are you, angel?"

"That birth stuff hurts, miss. Missus. Freakin' hurts."

"Yeah, I've heard. Totally worth it, though?" I asked, touching the baby on the head.

Jacky's eyes teared. "Oh yeah. Way. You want to hold Dah-lee?" She said the name awkwardly. Drawn out, isolating the syllables.

"Yes, I do. Boy or girl?" I asked.

"We're not sure yet. We'll have to ask Dah-lee when the time is right."

"Oh, I see, a gender-neutral baby. Until you need some help changing those diapers."

"It's not a secret. Dah-lee has the anatomy of a girl. So you can change the diaper if it's necessary." I lifted the baby from her, and she lowered her hospital gown quickly over her exposed breast. "Freaking hurts," she repeated, rubbing her breast. "What the hell, I thought that yesterday would be the worst of it, but my boobs have been singing the blues for eight months, and now it's just going to get worse? Not fair."

"Really, that tough on the girls, huh?" I'd never thought of that.

"No, not really, just the first trimester really bad. That's how I first knew. Got naked, and my boobs looked like damn cantaloupes. Until now. Now, like, basketballs." She continued to massage herself. I lowered my eyes to the baby's face, embarrassed, and watched as the unseeing eyes opened, and the face yawned mightily.

"Not any better, love?" someone asked from the door. My eyes, darting from the apple-sized face, found its exact replica there in the door. Smiling, dewy eyed, looking so full at Jacky and then the baby in my arms. A proud father.

"Nuh-uh," Jacky answered. "Don't be rude, Jason, say hello to Mrs. Harmon."

"Hi, Mrs. Harmon. It's good to see you."

"Thanks, Trixie. It's good to be back."

"Peter, can you throw the clothes in the dryer?" I asked, but I wasn't sure if he could hear me over the coffee grinder. At least I couldn't hear his inevitable question. Marrying a man in his mid-thirties is not different at all from marrying a twelve year old if he has been as thoroughly spoiled as Peter. He may not have believed in Santa Claus for a long time, but he still believed in the laundry fairy, who washed, dried, ironed or folded his clothes and returned them to their proper drawers and closets in the correct color pattern arrangement.

"Peter, did you hear me?" I turned off the grinder.

"What?" he said, popping into the kitchen.

"Put the clothes in the dryer, please," I said, dumping the coffee into the filter.

"Why?"

"So we can have dry clothes instead of wet, mildewy ones," I answered.

"I never had to dry clothes before," he stated, not whining, just factual.

265

"I know, but I don't think your sister will do your laundry anymore. You can ask. Let me know how that goes. Will you put this one last load in the dryer, though, before she takes over again?"

"What do I set it on?"

"Dry, I guess. Go?" I wasn't sure. I hadn't done much of my own laundry.

"Do I need one of those sheets?"

"Yes, add one of those." I pushed the button on the coffeemaker and turned and walked to the bathroom to dry my hair and end the conversation. But he followed me. I turned the hair dryer to high and leaned over to blow the underlayers of my hair, but my breasts throbbed with my impending cycle or my husband's increasingly comfortable manipulation. Peter didn't move. He watched my boobs swing as I stood up. "Honey, if you don't start the dryer, I'm going to have to go to school naked. You wouldn't like that would you?"

He went to the laundry room, but was back in seconds. I put on my robe. "Do you need dryer sheets if you use this?" He held the fabric softener bottle.

"No, probably not. Just start it without one," I said, slapping on my make-up.

"Then why'd you tell me we needed one? This is for downy softness, and the other is for bounciness. Are those the same thing? I kind of thought they were about smell. Or, no really, static energy suppression. Which one does that? Both?"

"I don't know, Peter, put it in or not, just dry the damn clothes."

"Okay, so then both?"

"Yes, it won't hurt to have both." I turned to the mirror. Adding blush seemed ridiculous when my face was flushed with frustration. Mascara. Coffee. I needed coffee.

I poured myself a cup and sat across from Peter. He was a beautiful man. He woke up scruffy and whiney, put on his running shoes and came back from his morning run as pleased with life as a long-tailed puppy.

I kissed his head. "Thanks for taking care of the laundry."

"I've never done laundry before," he said again.

"I know, and soon you won't have to anymore, but until I finish this school year, I'm going to need help with that stuff. Just a few more weeks, right?" I sat down across from him with my coffee.

"I've got to run. It's dental day," he said. Once a month or so, they scheduled a day full of feline teeth cleaning for him. It was another miserable job, but he could deal pretty well with the cats as long as they were sedated. And he had a weapon.

He kissed me good bye. Our coffee breath blending seemed more like married than anything else I could imagine. The first several weeks after our return from the honeymoon, these good-bye kisses were dangerous. We'd both called in horny a number of times as the kisses led us back to the bedroom.

Krista was a pro at the morning routine now, and Paula was more tolerant than either of us had anticipated. In fact, the first time, he'd made me call her. But that was the only time. Once I got her on the phone, I told her that I'd lost the keys to the handcuffs, and Peter would remain bound to the trapeze until I located it. After that, he would call her himself. Once he'd said that my cervical mucus consistency seemed to indicate that I was ovulating. She requested that he forgo the call in the future and just do his best to arrive on time, since his bedroom was about 20 yards from work, she couldn't see that it would be that difficult. Shows what she knows.

I drained my coffee, and turned off the Today Show right after the headlines, my cue to get dressed and head to school. As I walked into the laundry room, the dryer finally came to a stop and buzzed. Inside my entire go-to-school wardrobe, along with every pair of panties I owned, were tumbled, and mostly dry. I pulled a pair of underpants out of the dryer, and some jeans. Mmmm, spring fresh, I thought, Peter must have thrown a few of those sheets in there. I grabbed a t-shirt out of the dryer and threw it on, pulling it over my head. I felt a smear down my back.

Grabbing the shirt off my back, I saw a bluish Rorschach blotch across the back of my shirt. Downy, which Peter had measured precisely, I'm sure, and poured into the dryer.

I put the clothes in a basket, and put them on Peter's side of the bed, not that we kept to our sides, but at the time, I certainly felt like keeping to myself tonight.

My back was already itching as the goo dried flaky down my back. I called Krista, "I'm jumping in the shower to wash the sticky off," I said as soon as she answered the phone, "but it's not as much fun as it sounds."

In the shower, I ripped the loofah off its hook and reached around to scrub at my back. Dummy, I thought, he's a doctor? I took my dying, now dead, cat to him and he's unable to even use simple fabric softener? My back soothed with the warm water, I turned away to scrub it heartily with the sponge, I wanted to preserve my face and hair, which were already prepared for the day. Instead, the water hit my neck but sprayed up, drizzling my face. Damn him.

I stepped back, and the warm water, suddenly shards, assaulted my breasts, and I doubled, automatically shielding them like I'd been punched in the stomach, sending my face then my hair right into the stream. I turned around and let the water rinse my back. I looked down, dazed still, trying to determine the source of the pain. Surely a previously unnoted raw open wound had been bombarded by the somehow acidic water. I shut off the tap with my elbow, without turning around. My breasts looked like a map of the Mississippi delta, all blue veins lacing across the land of my more than normal bulbous boobs.

I put back on the Downy splotched shirt, and the jeans too, over my still wet body, and ran across to the clinic. Inside the surgery, Peter was perched on the far examining table looking toward the tabby on the table nearest the door. "You're sure he's out?" he said tremulously. I slammed the door and the kitty didn't move, but the vet technician did, straight up in the air.

I grabbed Peter, pulled him off the table toward me. His legs wrapped around my waist and I spun him.

"Daddy!" I said, crying. Then shouted, "Daddy! You are going to be a daddy!" I joggled him up and down as he screamed, which looked obscene, I'm sure.

Paula came running in, a goopy eyed Cocker spaniel and its owner behind her. I dropped my husband. "We're pregnant!" I screamed, and hugged her, and the owner, and the Cocker spaniel and the vet tech.

"I'm having Peter's baby!" I said, and then it was too much. I fell to my knees and Peter ran to me, still smiling, and dropped down beside me. "Your baby, I'm going to have your baby. There's going to be another you," I said in total wonderment, with—for the first time in my life—a true humility and gratitude at the miracle that was God and love and life. I got to make another Peter Harmon. I hugged him, sobbing, "I get to have another you," I said into his neck and again into his chest and lap, as I fell down and down on the surgery floor. Truly prone, prostrate and worshipful both of my God who had made the man, and the man who represented my God, just as Mama had promised.

"Glory be to the Father, and to the Son, and to the Holy Spirit. As it was in the beginning, is now, and ever shall be, world without end. Amen." I'm not sure who said it. It was Paula, or the spaniel owner, but it was the last thing I heard before the sobbing started. It was Paula, and then it was me. For very different reasons. Or the same one: there would be another Peter.

Krista had spent the entire day with Mama, which had made both of them a wreck. When Manny, Peter, and I arrived, we brought wine, and we were all friends again within the hour. Except for me. My ankles looked more like my thighs, and I was still reliving my traumatic morning. And I, of course, could not have wine.

I had stepped out of the shower, and Peter's eyes, drawn to my belly, had cried, "Oh my God, what have you done to yourself?" grabbing a towel and pressing it against my belly as against a wound.

"What are you doing? Get off me," I said.

"Why?" he panted, pulling the towel off to inspect it. Confused, he looked at me. "You hurt yourself?"

"What are you talking about?" I walked to the closet doors, full length mirrors. On the downhill side of my belly, below the beltline, down to my pubic bone, were raw reddish purple worms, fault lines. "You boob, Peter, they're stretch marks. Jesus, I'm six months pregnant."

"I didn't know. I'm sorry. They're normal then? Pretty awful-looking, are you sure that's normal?" He jabbed one finger at a purply crevice. It sunk in. "It looks like Geopoliticus Child."

"I don't know what that is." God I was cranky.

"It's a painting. Salvador Dali," he said and took a deep breath to elaborate, but I was not in the mood.

"What did you think?" I cut in, slapping his hand away.

"I thought you'd cut yourself," he said. "Like trying to cut, you know. Cut the—," he dropped his eyes.

"Get out, I've got to get dressed," I had said, and I still held onto my rage. I may not have had a model's body. Ever. I never even had hips, really, until now. The differences in my body, so severe, so sudden, so misshapen, made me mourn my more simplistically straight figure.

Of course, I would get it back, but now I had these lovely stretch marks to remember this more full-figured Ellie. When I'd gone to get my single cup of coffee, (which I drank each morning under Peter's watchful eye while he admonished, only once per day, "I don't think you should be drinking coffee while we're pregnant,") Peter had given me my new nickname. I was now Ellie the Belly.

Even though I'd broken into tears when he said it, he still repeated it to the congregated party at the baby shower. Mom and Manny were drunk enough by then to laugh; Krista, though, was either not drunk enough or sane even through her fog to wince.

She continued to cringe every time he called me "Belly." When one of Mom's Rosary club ladies asked how far along I was and Peter answered her, "We are starting the third trimester next week," Krista had finally had enough.

"You are not pregnant, Peter," she said. "In case you haven't noticed, Ellie—not Belly—is the one carrying the child."

Before Peter could answer, Krista stood up and walked down the hall toward the bathroom. Peter continued opening the gift he was unwrapping. "An electric double breast pump with a harness!" he said enthusiastically, and began reading the packaging. "It has a comfortable flexi-fit, so quiet only you will know you're pumping! Small and discreet."

"Just like you," Manny said, and he got up, got a beer from the refrigerator, and left down the hall.

"I bet we could hook this up to some compressed air and pump even faster," Peter continued gushing.

"How about a game?" Mama said coming in from the kitchen. She and Krista had spent some time researching fun baby shower games. "This is the Dirty Diaper game," she began handing out little slips of paper to record our guesses and little pink and blue pencils.

On TV trays, Mom had laid out tiny little diapers with melted chocolate bars mushed into them. We were to determine the name of the candy by appearance, smell, and taste if we were brave enough. I took one look at the Reese's diaper and felt the dozen or so tiny quiches I'd eaten rising. I ran for the bathroom.

Mama kept all the doors closed to keep Worf from wandering around claiming everything as his, and the closed door slowed me down enough that by the time I entered the restroom and saw naked Krista straddling my brother on the bathroom counter, I was already spewing vomit.

Peter was happy enough to leave me behind with Mama so we could write thank-you cards. And everyone else was downright eager to leave after the vomit sprinkler, not to mention the unintentional free peepshow they'd seen when they'd come to check on me. Instead of thank-you cards, though, we brought out two decks of playing cards and set in to play canasta.

I thought I might actually be able to beat her since she'd had a few glasses of wine. "You still throwing up a lot, this far along?" Mom asked.

"No, not daily or anything," I said, shifting in my seat. "But I still have the hemorrhoids, the swollen ankles, acid reflux, and beautiful stretch marks."

"Sounds like you're having a great time," she laughed. "Y'all gonna' do this again?"

"I can't even imagine. I'm too old, but if that's what God has planned. We won't prevent it, if that's what you're asking." I sighed. When would I ever graduate from catechism class?

"Don't get snippy, missy, I was just making conversation. And there are natural ways to prevent pregnancy, you know."

"Yeah, we learned all about the rhythm method in our marriage-prep class," I laughed. "Not that reliable."

"There's always abstinence," Mom said quietly. I threw down my cards.

"God, Mama, why are we having this conversation? Do you have some objection to my having a child? A husband? A sex life?" I was yelling now, and the tears began. Mine and hers.

"Ellie, honey, I'm sorry. I was just—I just wanted to talk to you. Tell you." She sighed, and laid down her cards.

"I had a really easy pregnancy with you," she started softly. "And you were such a good baby. So happy, and smart. We wanted a dozen, just like you. As soon as my doctor gave us the go-ahead, we started trying again. Whenever you outgrew something, I'd wash it and fold it and put it in the dresser in the 'nursery' ready for the next one to use it. Then we had to buy another dresser, and another. Finally I put all your little things into storage," Mama started crying a little again.

"Oh, it used to make me so mad when people would tell me to be happy with what I had. I was grateful. I am grateful, but I just, well, I guess I felt that God didn't think we were fit enough parents. Here you were, about ready to start school, and nothing. Then, finally, I was pregnant.

"Oh, we were so happy. Brought out all those baby things. But I wasn't good into my second trimester when I started spotting. Doctor said it was normal.

Nothing to worry about. But I miscarried. Never again, I said." She got up and got a dishtowel to wipe her face. She stood there, looking out the sink window into the backyard. To the shed. "And you know the rest. We abstained, until one day, your daddy just lost it. And we had Manny. I had Manny. He was gone before he really knew."

She looked at me, but her eyes did not look hollow and distant, like I'd expected. Not even grieved. "I'm so sorry, Mama. I didn't know you'd lost a baby."

"Oh the worst part is all the babies we could have had, but didn't. All the blessings I missed."

"Don't be too hard on yourself, they may have all turned out like Manny, instead of me," I joked, but Mama wasn't ready.

"I didn't learn my lesson, though; look what I did to you. Thirty-three years old. You could have had twelve kids by now," she laughed. "But I couldn't stand for you to face the grief."

I put my hands protectively over my belly. "I've had a perfectly normal pregnancy, Mom. Just the normal discomforts."

"Oh, I know. You were meant for bearing babies," she smiled. "I meant that other thing. Seeing someone you love so much. Seeing them change. That's hard. Your daddy was a good man."

"I know, Mom, I remember," I went to her and hugged her to me. "You guys were great together."

"I know. We were. And I was going to tell him so. Tell him that it was okay. We were going to have a baby."

I led her back to the table, sat her down, and knelt in front of her, like looking into the face of a child. "I'm so sorry, Mama. So sorry you lost him. We lost him. But, as you always used to tell me, everything happens for a reason. God's grand plan. You didn't cause me to lose those years, you helped me make myself ready for Peter, the only one I was supposed to be with. We both needed that time. To grow up.

"Well, for me to grow up. For Peter to learn some social skills. So, really, we probably could have waited a few more years even. Maybe he could have learned to do laundry too." I lifted myself into the chair beside Mama and took her hand. "Did I ever tell you how Peter and I met?" I asked. "Not at the football game, I know you heard that one. But the first time, back in high school? I didn't remember until Peter told me.

"It was the first day of school, and his first day at our school ever, and we were waiting out front of the school, I was with my little group of friends, flirting with the football team, and they started picking on this funny looking kid. Big old briefcase, looked like a trumpet case. The football players took it away from him, opened it up and started rifling through it. This poor short skinny kid just stood there looking at them. Crying.

"So I went over there, and slammed that thing shut on their fingers. Broke the quarterback's middle finger, so I was supposedly responsible for our 7-3 season. Twisted up one of the boy's arms until he apologized to the kid. Peter."

"Oh, I remember, Ellie. Getting suspended the first day of your senior year. Before the first bell even rang. Yes, I remember."

"It was for a good cause. It was just the beginning," I said. "Mama, what was Daddy like? When you were pregnant with me?"

"Well at first he treated me like I was made of egg shells and spider webs. Wouldn't let me do nothing. Then when I got big, he kept his head or hand on my belly ever second. I thought I might have to go to work with him so he wouldn't miss a single kick. And sang

281

'Top of the World' to you, and you know how your daddy was, he couldn't sing good so he sang loud, like you were in a sound-proof room several blocks away."

"Peter isn't like that, Mama. He doesn't seem to care—or almost to even know that there's a little person in here." I rubbed my belly. "Today was the first time he's ever shown any excitement since he first found out. And I think he just liked opening presents."

"I don't know, Ellie, think about how he seems to think that he's pregnant too."

"Yeah, but, I still feel like I'm having this baby alone. He doesn't want to talk about names, or themes for the nursery, or anything like that."

"It's still abstract to him, Ell. When he sees that baby, he will know. He will change then."

The baby stuck one of its fourteen elbows into my ribs. "Well it is certainly a concrete concept to me," I said.

Since the day of the shooting I'd parked on the other side of the school so I could get to my room without passing the ISS room, which was now used as an out-of-adoption-book closet. But I'd used the excuse of my pregnancy to park close again, and walking by the room was not as bad as I'd anticipated.

Of course when I passed it, it was normally at a full on run since I was so reluctant to get out of bed in the mornings, and it had nothing to do with a warm and happy husband. I was just so tired.

Peter had found that there were two ways to get me out of bed. One was morning sickness. The second was setting his phone alarm to sound like a doorbell, which made Worf insane, which then made it impossible for anyone to sleep since his barking stirred up the boarding dogs. The neighbors were not any more fond of this technique than I was, but I bet they got to work on time too.

The stairs were also no friend of mine. Every time I took a step up, I could feel the fluid in my ankles slosh. But Mama was right, I was built for bearing babies, at over 6 feet tall I provided plenty of room for the baby to stretch out, so I did not have the big mound of a belly that some women had at twenty-eight weeks.

Krista was in the room, cutting out feathers and headbands for our Indians. I had the Pilgrim hats to finish before the bell rang. No problem. "Hey, Pretty Mama, how are you doing this morning?"

"Grrr," I said. "Where's my freaking glow that I'm supposed to have by this point?"

"You're glowing," she said.

"No, I'm sweating. It's going to be 90 degrees today. In November. It's ridiculous."

"You are just a ray of sunshine this morning," Krista said.

"Sorry," I said, "I actually don't feel bad at all. I'm just sad."

"Hormones?" Krista measured the brown construction paper strip around her head and the stapled it.

"No," I sighed. "I know this is shocking, but it's Peter."

Krista smiled. She listened to so much of my marital complaining that she had resurrected the suggestion of a mobster convict husband more than once. She'd even offered to visit her ex-boyfriend in prison to scope out prospects. "What happened?"

"Nothing," I said. "That's the problem. I think Peter was over the idea of having a baby as soon as he finished opening his presents. There's no excitement in planning, or picking names, or feeling the little imp kick my ribs out of place. He just doesn't care. I have no one to share my happiness or my fear with."

"Surely Peter is interested in something," she said.

"Oh, he is. He's interested in measuring the depth, width, and color of my stretch marks, and the size of my boobs, and when my belly will get big enough for me to give in and do it doggy style."

"You're still doing it?"

"I have to. It's in the pre-nuptial agreement."

"You signed a pre-nup?"

"No," I answered, "it's more like a gentleman's agreement. He'll pay the mortgage, I'll buy the groceries. I'll cook, he'll do the dishes. Sexual relations will be had at least one time per

285

week, except in the case of illness if there is a doctor's note."

"Does he get to write his own note?"

"I don't foresee his abstaining, even if he had dysentery."

"Is it awful?" she asked. "No, I'm sorry, I shouldn't have asked, I don't want to know."

"Yes you do."

"Okay, I do, but I still shouldn't have asked."

"No, it's not awful. It's not even bad. In fact, the orgasms tend to calm the baby."

"Orgasms? You have orgasms with someone else in the room? You bitch," Krista said, finishing her head bands and rolling my pilgrim hats into cylinders.

"You don't?" I asked, honestly confused. I kind of thought that was the point.

"No, never," she said.

"Hmm, maybe my husband needs to talk with my brother."

"Yeah, maybe." I glued the paper buckles onto the hats. "But, back to the point, you didn't get pregnant alone, and now you have to be pregnant alone and that sucks. Maybe your brother should have a talk with your husband. Manny's very excited about the baby. He even talks about having one himself someday."

"You explained that it's impossible, right?"

"Yeah, we've discussed the necessary process."

The hats were finished when the bell rang. We put the hats and headdresses away. Today's language arts lesson would be some exciting readers' theatre, but there was no reason to start the whining during morning check-in and goal setting.

Trixie and Trevor came in together, friends now that Trevor had proof that Trix was a "guy," although Trixie's rainbow colored bumper sticker said "Mom." Brian came in alone, a sad statement that not even the NPJ's would hang out with him. Over the summer he'd been adjudicated for exposing himself in the park to some little kids, so he was a pariah even here.

Walter had been showing up almost as late as Becca, who had to count the lockers to order her world on the way to school. They would be here soon.

Nathan had been mainstreamed into regular classes, the support he got coming from me after school on our way to the clinic. Jacky had managed to graduate, her happy but tense family looking on: Daddy, some aunts and cousins, and Trixie holding the baby Dolly/Dali. Munch, of course, was in

Huntsville's maximum security prison for the rest of his natural life.

Our newest freshmen, Ashley and Levi, were a very unique set. Twins. Ashley was a cutter; she left a trail of blood wherever she went, like Ted Bundy, but it was her own blood. Her scarred arms looked like she was creating a very intricate tartan. Levi, a pathological liar, explained that he and his twin, having been kidnapped as toddlers, grew up in a remote South American village where the kind of body modification his twin practiced was normal for the maidens. Trevor had pointed out that she was very likely to maintain her maidenhood for a while, and he hoped there would be something left to deflower when the time came for her to be relieved of her maidenhead.

Becca came slamming in through the door, obviously agitated. Finger going from nose to chest to nose to chest furiously.

"Becca, what's going on, sweetie?" I was thinking maybe someone left a locker open, disrupting her count. It happened from time to time.

"Mrs. Harmon, I need to talk to you, in private. Right now," she said firmly.

"Okay," I looked toward the red square.

"No, really in private."

"It's cool," Krista said, "I can start with the goal setting."

"Let's go to the lounge, sweetie," I said, "You want to leave your books here?" She was clutching them to her chest like a shield.

"No," she answered tersely. "Let's go."

She ran out the door, and I followed her out. "What is going on?" I asked, struggling to keep up. She headed for the stairs.

"I can't tell you out here. I don't want him to hear. He said he would—"

She stopped when Walter rounded the corner of the landing and stood just two steps below us. He could still look down at Becca, and see me almost eye to eye. Becca grabbed my arm. We kept moving, past him.

"It's okay," I whispered. Then louder, "Thanks for helping get the supplies, Bec, I don't feel like I should be lifting anything too heavy right now."

"I could help," Walter said, stopping.

"Thanks, but it's nothing this strong woman can't handle." I put my arm around Becca's shoulders, and I could feel her shaking. "Let's go," I said, but I felt her stumble just a little.

"Remember what I said," he said softly, his voice almost casual, and

Becca's knees buckled. We turned the corner around the landing.

I moved my arm to her waist and lifted her down to the next step. "Move your feet," I whispered, but Walter had turned around and jumped back down to the landing and she tried to step down and away from him. He grabbed the back of her shirt. "Walk, Becca," I said, and she tried to move her feet but only managed to stumble over them. She fell, and I fell with her. It was just a few steps, but with my arm holding Becca, I did not do a good job of breaking my fall. The Whale, intent on Becca, followed. He landed on me, which made it easy for me to restrain him.

I locked my arms around his in a full nelson, clasping my hands firmly behind his head. "Go to the room. Tell Miss Parker to call the SRO." I tried to make eye contact with her, allow her to see my urgency. The baby kicked hard enough that the boy in my grasp felt it too. "Go, Becca."

There was nothing I could do spooning a corpulent juvenile, and there was very little he could do, lying on his side with his arms locked over his head, but he screamed and cursed, and finally rolled backward onto me. Becca ran, finally, up the stairs, screaming for Krista.

"What were you doing to her?"

"Nothing," he said. "I can't breathe."

"*You* can't breathe, fatso? I got a whale on me, you know."

"My mom is so gonna' hear about this," he sat up a little, as much as he had ever done a sit-up in his life, and slammed down back onto me. My head, not clear of the bottom step, hit it hard. When I came back to myself, he was gone.

There was a very young man above me, he smelled very good and had short hair. He had a uniform. Krista's face appeared behind him, "Ellie, do you know what happened? Did you fall?"

"The Whale was going to hurt Bec. Keep them apart. Who's with the kids?"

"They're here," and they were, lined up on either side of the fire drill rope, clasping it and looking horror stricken. I lifted my head. I had heavy blankets on me, I could feel their weight.

The children were standing in a puddle of blood. I started to scream. At least no one understood, "Munch, Munch. Jesus Christ, it's Munch!" I tried to get up, but they held me down. There was a needle and there was finally silence.

27

"Your Nurse is," but the space underneath it was blank. "Just dial," and that space was blank too. The room was minty green, with a yellow and lavender couch. It was the maternity ward.

The blinds were drawn against the street lights. Nighttime, but the lights were on, bright overhead. The room was big. A birthing room. I took inventory of my body. Did I give birth? There was an uncomfortable wideness in my hips. Like after the fake honeymoon. There was a heating pad maybe on my back. My butt was soggy.

"Mama?" I said, but I knew there would be no answer. There was not a sound. Not a sound anywhere. "Mama!" I yelled. "Mama! Come get me! Mama!"

Mama did not come, but someone did, and soon it did not matter who it was or wasn't.

The street lights were out, but the light was not assaultive when I woke next. Someone was crying. I closed my eyes and pretended to sleep for a short period before I actually did, so I wouldn't learn who it was. I thought it might be me.

The next time I saw the street lights through the blinds, I heard Peter's voice, "I'm here for you," but I couldn't turn toward it before my mind fell against the monitor. Was it mine? Or my baby's? But I was asleep.

"Mama?" I said, and it was a real question. I hadn't seen my mother outside of her house and the church since I was able to drive. Sixteen years of on the couch, in the pew, or in the passenger seat.

"I'm so sorry, Eloise," she said. She said my whole name. "Not just for me, but for you and Peter too," and she buried her head in my belly. It was softer, more giving than when Peter had done it on our wedding day. My belly gave. In. It gave in.

I put my hand in her hair. Mama. Mother. She was sorry. For me. For Peter. The baby was gone. That was the wideness I felt. The emptiness of my baby.

———

Krista was there next time reading to me from the get-well-soon cards the kids had sent.

"Hey," I said.

"Hey, you're awake," she said and put the cards down.

"How long have I been asleep?"

"Not long, really. You've been in and out for two days," she looked at her watch. "Two and a half."

"You went to school?"

"Yeah, just got out and came over here."

"How's Becca?"

"Ellie, do you know why you're here?"

Peter opened the door, hidden behind a spray of sunflowers, orange roses, artful willowy sticks, and yellow kangaroo paws.

"I'm going to go," Krista said and picked up my hand, kissed my fingers.

"No, Becca?"

"She's fine. The Whale asked her out. That's all. He didn't want her to tell that he got turned down."

"Where's he?"

"Jail, Ellie," Krista looked confused. She kissed my hand again and kissed Peter's cheek as she went by. He was still hiding behind the flowers.

"Hey, how's my favorite guy?" He peeked around the bouquet, his eyes resting on my belly.

"Fine," he said.

"Oh, good, so you've seen him?"

"Who?" he asked.

"Peyton Manning. My favorite guy."

"I think he's still out. Out for the season."

"Yeah, I think so too. Come here, second favorite guy."

Peter put the flowers down on the bedside table, and pulled up a rocker with a cushy yellow seat. He touched my hand, but hit the IV, so he laid his hand on my arm. His hands were freezing. "Belly," he started softly. "Ellie," he tried again. He moved his hand down to my stomach, and I tried to put my hand on his, but I couldn't move it. I noticed for the first time that it was in a cast.

"I broke my arm?"

"Yes, but I think you had some help."

"I don't remember anything. Tell me, Peter," I said.

"Don't make me, Ellie. I can't," he pulled his hand away and covered his face.

"It's your job, honey. You have to. Tell me." I thought of Nathan spray painting the field house, and Paula saying that he did what he was told. I wanted to put my hand on his head, or touch his shoulder, or just say his name. But I couldn't. "Do it. From the beginning."

295

"You and that really big kid were on the stairs in a restraint. He rolled over on you, and hurt your," he touched my stomach. He continued robotically. "The uterus ruptured or something, and your arm was broken from the struggle somehow. The ulna, it's called a nightstick fracture, usually caused by impact, so you probably hit it on a step or the railing. Maybe the door. Krista came down with the kids, and walkied for an ambulance. You asked for your mother. She called Manny and then me." He stopped, breathed.

"Airedale, bitchin' frizzy," I started.

"Bichon frise," he corrected.

"Chow chow."

"Thanks," he said, "Dandie Dinmont, English mastiff. You were in surgery when I got here. There was no fetal heartbeat; they tried a cesarean, but it was too late. The uterus had been ruptured. They had to take it. Fetal demise."

"Fetal demise?"

"Perinatal loss."

"Peter, tell me."

"It was a boy, he would have been perfect. He had little eyelashes. But he was dead."

"You saw him? Where is he? I want to see him." I tried to sit up but the emptiness turned rageful and I had to lie back. "Bring him to me." Peter put his hand on my arm.

"There's been a necropsy. No, autopsy."

"Is that son of a bitch in jail? The Whale? That fucker. Murderer!"

"No, Ellie, listen."

"I want him. I want him dead. Just like my son. Dead, dead, dead. Murdering retard. Damned piece of shit, damn him."

"Ellie, stop. You have to stop."

But I couldn't, I was screaming and ripping at the sheets, slapping at Peter when he tried to touch me, comfort me.

"Ellie, he didn't do it. It wasn't him. It was you, your body. He didn't kill the baby, the baby died. Your uterus should have been able to protect him, and maybe it would have under normal circumstances, but it didn't. It's called incompetent uterus. He's a child, Ellie."

"He's not a child, he's a dead baby," I screamed.

"No, honey, The Whale, just a kid."

"Get out, get out, I hate you!" I found, finally, the nurse's call button, and within seconds of punching at it like an over-eager Jeopardy contestant, the door burst open and the nurse came in, followed closely by my mother.

"Frances," Peter said to Mom, "I didn't mean to. She made me tell her."

The nurse injected something into the IV, and Mama closed the door after Peter.

We decided on just a graveside service for our son. Manny drove Mama and me there from the hospital. I stood beside Peter as Father Nguyen prayed, and we said good-bye to the child Peter had named Francis Warden Harmon. I hugged Paula and Nathan, and Peter left with them.

"Go with your husband," Mama insisted, blocking my way to the car. "It is your duty. You chose it." She wouldn't let me in. She'd told me on the way from the hospital that the expectation was that I would go home to Peter's house. "He needs you," she told me. "He lost a baby too."

"No, he didn't. He lost the idea of a baby. It wasn't real to him."

So I got in Krista's car, and told her to make sure we arrived at Mom's house before Manny so Mama couldn't keep me locked out of her house too. Krista told me that the Rosary ladies had prepared a full Thanksgiving meal and had it ready at "the family home."

"I'm going home, Krista."

"No, your home. Yours and Peter's. My God, you can be a selfish bitch," she told me, refusing, at first, to help me out of the car and into the house. Finally, she grabbed my unbroken arm and wrapped it around her shoulder and dragged me up the front stairs. She left me there, digging in my purse for my keys. "I'm going to have some turkey."

"Great. Happy Thanksgiving. I'm glad you have so much to celebrate."

"You do too, damn you."

"Yep, a dead baby, and no possibility of carrying another one, dead or alive. And a husband who blames me or my incompetent body. Happy Thanksgiving."

Before they got home, I'd chewed up two Xanax and settled on the couch with my old Snuggie that I hadn't taken when I moved to Peter's. I was pulling Edna's hairs off of it, and laying them out in a row on the arm of the sofa when Mama, Manny and Krista came in.

"We brought you a plate," Mama said sighing. "You stubborn fool."

"Thanks, Mom," I said, sincerely.

"And we brought you something else." Mama sat on the other end of the couch in her designated spot, shoving my feet aside. I sat up, and she put a little blue box down between us. It had a little angel on it.

"No," I said. "I don't want to." I tried to get up, but the Snuggie, and Xanax, hindered my progress. And being stitched together from hip to hip probably didn't help.

Manny and Krista sat in the floor in front of me; Krista laid her head against my knees, and Manny held her hand, and then took mine too.

"Sis, you've got to do this."

"Forget you, Manny, what do you know? How many babies have you killed? You never cared. How could you understand?"

"I don't. I won't. I can't. You're right. But you've got to try to understand."

"What am I missing? My baby is dead because I couldn't protect him. Plus I made a terribly risky decision. I've had a ridiculous year. School shooting, Edna's death, my son's death."

"Falling in love, getting married, starting a life," Krista said, and I saw her squeeze Manny's hand.

Mom opened the box. There was the baby's birth certificate. We'd never decided on a name. Francis Warden at the cemetery was the first I'd heard of it. Peter said he wasn't good at that kind of thing. He'd only suggested Jetson, as in George Jetson. And Valentine from *Stranger in a Strange Land*.

"Francis," I said. Of course it was perfect, but I could also hear him saying something like "no use wasting a good name on a dead baby."

A tear fell onto the paper, and Krista sopped it off with her sleeve, and handed me the next item, the tiniest little footprint. His tiny little toes, with his own little whorls, in baby blue on cream colored card stock.

Mama handed me a little photo album covered in blue gingham fabric with a little ribbon. "Our Angel" was embroidered on the cover.

The first picture was of Peter holding Francis, obviously in the operating room, just after delivery. He was blue. My husband was bowed so low over the baby that their foreheads almost touched, and both their faces were in the shadow.

I could see Francis's face in the next photo, a close-up with Peter's finger touching the baby's downy face, his finger longer than his son's face. I could see his little eyelashes.

Then, in the room where I woke up, the silly lavender plaid couch in the background, Peter held Francis over a stainless steel mixing bowl with Father Nguyen, the christening. And finally Peter, his face contorted and wet, handing the baby to Mom.

Inside the box, was a christening gown, never worn and much too big for the baby. "Peter's?" I asked.

"Yes, he put all this together. That was his gown," Mama said.

"He was a big baby," I said.

"He still is," Krista said.

There was also a pregnancy journal in the box. The kind that mothers-to-be use to record their morning sickness, proposed names, cravings, hopes and thoughts. Every page, up to twenty-seven weeks, was full. A tally of how many times I'd vomited each day since May. Cravings for cheddar cheese and green chilies. Belly measurements, and the week-by-week photos. In the margins of the journal, there were facts and graphics, statistics, and quotations. Some of them Peter had highlighted or drawn a little happy face. At the fifteen week mark, when down, called lanugo, covers the baby, Peter had drawn a little monkey beside the "Factoid!" box.

The last entry, the twenty-seventh week, Peter had written, "The joys of parents are secret, and so are their griefs

and fears. Francis Bacon." The page
was warped as if left in the rain.

29

"Eloise," Mama hollered from the kitchen. "Get your butt out here right now. I'm not gonna serve cold food at my table."

Mama had made breakfast. A real breakfast. I'd heard the bacon crackling, and the soft thwack, puh, thwack, puh of Mama cutting out the biscuits with a jelly jar and plopping them onto the baking sheet. I'd been served the desiccated cat rectums for the previous two days that I'd been holed up in my old bedroom, and I hadn't eaten a thing. She had a good plan. I loved me a farmer's breakfast. "Coming, Ma," I said, pulling my hair out of my eyes in a sloppy one-handed pony tail.

My body was stiff from lying in bed, but I wasn't as sore as I would have anticipated. My arm was itchy in the cast, but the incision across my belly was just a closed-lip smile, a little yellowed with bruising. "Ellie!" Mom prodded.

She handed me a cup of coffee before I'd even sat down at the table. "How are you feeling, baby?"

I smiled at her, if anyone knew, she did. "As good as can be expected," I said, and my vision blurred with tears. "I'm good. Getting there, at least."

"Your husband called. Sixty-four times, I think."

"What are you telling him?"

"That, although you are acting like a self-centered two year-old, you are grieving and so not thinking clearly. Give you some time."

"Thanks, Mama," I said, tearing my biscuit into bite size pieces before I drowned it with gravy. "What did they tell you when you lost the baby? I mean, what was the reason?"

"They didn't know. Never said."

"Have you ever heard the term 'incompetent uterus?'"

"Oh, yeah, I think that's what they say any time there's a miscarriage. I thought it was incompetent cervix. Damn mean words, though, I'd say."

Woof-woof, Mama's guard dog barked. "Worf-Worf," Worf seemed to answer in his deep-chested growly voice. "Oh, Mama, really? Do we have to do this?"

"Yes, you do. We're in here, Peter!" Mama said, bringing out another plate, and a cold hamburger patty she must have fried up for Worf.

"Ellie, honey, how are you?" Peter asked, his eyes liquid, not the least bit remote or angry. And that's what I'd feared. Yes, I'd been selfish, grieving on my own, but I couldn't stand it if I saw accusation in his eyes.

"I'm sorry, Peter, I'm so sorry," I began to sob, and he lowered himself to his knees in front of me. Just like the day he'd proposed, right here at Mama's table.

"Oh, my angel," he said and hugged me close. He pulled back, held my face in his hands, and looked directly into my eyes for a long moment. For Peter, this was monumental. "Ellie, my darling wife, you smell like a Yeti. How long since you've had a shower?"

I laughed and swiped the tears away. "The nurse gave me a ho-bath at the hospital before the funeral."

"My love, you poor thing. How are you feeling?" He touched my belly.

"Sad. Devastated. Guilty. Weary. Hopeless."

"Wow, that's a lot."

"How are you feeling, Peter? Do you hate me?"

"Ellie, no. Jesus. No, no, no." And my husband cried unashamedly, his face in my lap, kneeling at my feet. "I am sad and guilty, and everything you said, but I don't blame you. Did you think I would blame you?"

Mom lit a cigarette. "Y'all ever had cold gravy? It ain't good."

"She's right, I'm starving," I said, turning to the table, needing the space, the reprieve. "You want me to butter a biscuit for you, Peter? You don't have to have gravy."

"Yes, please," he said, "but I've got to run to the car. I brought you something. I'll be right back, Beloved." I decided not to tell him right then that *Beloved* was one of my favorite novels; it's about a woman who murders her infant. "Come on, Worf."

"Thanks, Mama, this is going to be hard. But like most stuff that's hard, it'll be worth it."

"Oh yes, Ellie, he's worth it. If he weren't, I wouldn't have let you marry him. And don't tell me that you can do what you want. We both know better. I saved you for him. We just didn't know it. Oh, wait, I forgot something." Mama jumped, ran to the door, and unplugged her woofing motion detector.

I shoveled a few bites of gravy and biscuits into my maw, out of sight of all who needed to believe me lady-like.

"Shh, be easy, Worf, gentle, gentle. Good boy," Peter coached the

Rottweiler through the living room into the dining room. The ninety pound dog walked like he was traveling on onion paper, tiptoeing toward me, with a red backpack like a saddle across him. "Stand, stand," Peter warned.

Peter rubbed his hand across his bald pate. He'd shaved, newly gleaming head and face. Some occasion, visiting the wife.

He pulled up a chair on the other side of Worf, the dog between us like a low table.

"Ellie, I am not a stupid man, but I say and do stupid things sometimes. Especially when saying and doing the right thing is crucial. But I want you to know, that today is not one of those times. I am doing the right thing. Not as a reaction, not to put my logical template over something that is not logical or knowable, like I did in the hospital with my foolish words and irrelevant explanations. But the right thing because in the quiet of my heart and mind, apart from the anxiety and pressure of the world that demands a right pre-conceived answer, I know what is right. For me, for you. Husband. It's a verb. To care for," he looked at Mama here.

"Close your eyes, Ellie," Mama said, like a kid who has waited too long for Christmas morning.

"Close your eyes," Peter repeated. I did, and I heard a zip, then another, and a gasp from Mama. "Here, my angel, my true love. Open your eyes."

Peter clutched two kittens to his chest. Two gorgeous furry kittens, paws like the feet of a wild hare, tails like boas. Maine coons.

"Ellie, may I present, Purrcivel and Meowhammad," he said, holding them out to me. Worf licked Meowhammad's face and he chirped, unoffended. Just like Edna.

"Peter, oh God, are you sure? Sure?"

"Yes, baby. I'm sure." I threw myself into his arms, careful not to squish the kittens with my cast.

"Thank you, Peter," I whispered, crying. I sat down on the dining room floor and took Purrcivel, a silver tabby, from him. He tucked his face into Meowhammad, a tuxedo kitty.

"They're actually pretty sweet," Peter said, sounding like a confused pre-schooler: what do you mean there's no Santa? But he turned serious quickly. "I know that kitties do not take the place of children. As much as we may love them, they can't mow the lawn, earn a 4.0 grade point average to validate us with our friends, or pay for a decent nursing home. And they are not children."

I wiped my tears on Purrcivel's fur then traded him for Meowhammad. "Thank you, Husband. They are beautiful."

"We can adopt. Or foster children. Or something," he said brightly, rubbing his own wet face into Purrcivel.

"Maybe. But for right now, we are all the family we need." I reached up and grabbed Mama's hand, but she held a balled wet paper towel in it, and I let it go.

"There's bacon," Mama said, her voice still thick with tears.

"Mmm, pig. The cutest animals taste the best," Peter said enthusiastically, and I shielded Purrcivel.

Within my first two days back home, I'd pulled Meowhammad down from the top of the curtains, out of the heating duct, and up from the garbage disposal, and it made me wonder how much fun it would have been to go through the terrible twos. Purrcivel had been rescued from the dryer and had gotten himself stuck in one of my Uggs. Worf delivered the Ugg to me with consternation. I thought he wanted to go for a winter wonderland walk, but with only his wildly flapping silver tail to alert us to the emergency, Purrcy set us straight.

Peter and I settled into the married life that we'd dreamed of, although there were nights when one or the other of us would wake up tearful and bereft. And there we would be, drinking coffee at 2:00 a.m. mourning the might-have-beens. I knew, though, that I would not let the tragedy of my little Francis ruin us. I always told my students that smart people learn from others' mistakes, and I had learned from my mother's.

Friday nights had become Hearts night at Mama's house; Mama and me versus Peter and Nannette. At least once every game, Meowhammad or Purrcivel would go skittering across the table, scattering cards and snacks and toppling drinks. But no one was bothered by this except Nannette.

Mom would invariably cuddle one of the kitties while Peter and I cleaned up the mess. "Y'all playing grab-ass on Granny's table?" she'd coo at them.

"Ay, Peter, why did you have to change your mind?" Nannette would fuss sincerely.

Finally, one night, trolling for popcorn kernels after a bowl-tossing incident, he explained. "You know I was afraid of cats. And I could never put my finger on why. I developed a theory when Paula brought home *All Cats Have Asperger's Syndrome*, but it was incomplete." Peter sat back on his heels, and absently let Worf lick the popcorn out of his hand.

"I thought that kitties were just untrustworthy. Sneaky and plotting. Then I heard Ellie describe her kids as Narcissistic Praise-Junkies, and I thought, 'Yeah, that's what it is.' Cats are just so wrapped up in themselves, but dogs are outgoing, easy to read. But dogs are too: egocentric, self-serving. See, that's the key. Dogs, cats, kids, adults, disabled, perfectly-abled. We're all just narcissistic praise-junkies. It's the way of the world.

"Otherwise, why would people have children, or write books, or do good deeds, or live worthy lives? Even if it's for God. It ends up being about heaven or hell. Recognition or rejection. So why be more scared of cats than of dogs? Or children or rodeo clowns or alligator gars? They're all the same. Should I pop some more popcorn, or are y'all ready for some s'mores?"

"Wow, Peter, that is truly inspiring. You should be a motivational speaker," Mama said.

"Do you think so, Frances? I think I would like that. You can be my agent."

While Mama oversaw Trixie and Jackie's decorating of the social hall, I had stuck painter's tape marks mid-wall along the back and side of the room. Our plan was for me to tug on Peter's pants leg when it was time to move from one blue tag to the next.

"Mrs. Harmon, those don't match at all, I'm afraid," Trixie had warned in her most tactful voice. She was excited to be a part of the decorating committee, but she had refrained from squealing. And she was right, the blue tape stood out obtrusively, but accommodations must be made.

"Do it, sugar," I told him after he'd finished his second round of the dog parade. That was enough warming up, I thought.

"Shit," he whispered.

"Shih-tzu, Tibetan mastiff, et cetera. Get up and go," I said, clinking my own glass with my knife. Peter stood and looked at the blue smear of tape on the eastern wall.

314

"Dear friends and family," he said and cleared his throat. I tugged on his pants leg and he transferred his eyes to the next tag. "I am humbled to serve as Manny's, and Ellie's, Best Man," he began with his rehearsed joke, and the crowd chuckled dutifully. "Had I known the expectations, however, I might have," I pulled his pants leg, "simply paid for a Las Vegas elopement." He took a drink of his ice water.

"All kidding aside, I have treasured the time that I have had getting to know my brother, Manny. Over the past few weeks, we've had some long and astute conversations about the meaning of love, of life, of marriage." Peter looked at Manny and then on to the next blue tag. "And I hope that I taught him as much as I learned. Not learned from him, of course, but from Ellie over the past year." Peter took another drink from his ice water. A long drink. He was maybe getting dehydrated from his excessive sweating. He looked down at his notes.

"And Krista, what a wonderful girl." Peter looked at the last one and then started over with the blue marks. "We didn't think anyone could tame Manny, or that anyone would actually want the full-time job of trying, so here's to you." I tugged frantically at his pants, until he looked at me and I nodded him toward Krista. He chuckled, embarrassed, and took another drink of water, but the glass, close to empty now, had to be tipped up precipitously.

The ice hitting his teeth and face, amplified over the microphone held too close, sounded like the cracking of the polar ice caps. The last of the water spilled out the sides of the glass, sides of his mouth, and drenched his chest. The lemon, perched on the side of the glass, stabbed Peter in the eye. When he dropped the glass, which shattered and sprayed Krista and me both with shards of glass and ice and water, the lemon stayed stuck in his now tightly closed eye.

"Abyssinian, Bengal, Cornish Rex, Devon Rex," his voice squealed over the microphone. I plucked the lemon out of his eye perhaps too exuberantly because he began to howl. And so did the audience. The laughter didn't reach me at first because I was so focused on Peter. But when he leaned over, whacking his head on the microphone, they roared, and I saw him as they did. As Jerry Lewis.

I handed him a glass of water, "Here, rinse out your eye," I whispered, but the microphone picked up my voice and echoed it. I grabbed the microphone before Peter had a chance to douse it. He looked straight ahead, like he was searching for one of those blue tags, and dumped the water energetically toward his right eye. Most of the water flew past him and drenched Krista, whose sheer wedding dress did not need any help with its transparency. Luckily, though, most of the deluge hit her upswept hair and flawless, until now, make-up.

Then Mama was there. She picked up the microphone and smacked it with her knuckles like she was a member of the SWAT team approaching a barred door. "Y'all hush, now," she said. I dabbed at Peter's reddened eye with a corner of my napkin soaked in water.

"Hush, I said," and when the crowd began to settle down, Mama continued. "Thank you, Peter, for that lovely speech and for baptizing Krista with that cleverly disguised holy water. We're terribly sorry about your blindness, but we will pray fervently for your restoration to health." The crowd and Peter, and Krista, laughed. Thank God.

"Allow me to finish up my dear son-in-law's sentiments," Mama continued. "Our family has grown again today, and we are truly blessed to have Krista and her mama join our happy troop," Mama raised the microphone like a toasting glass to Doreen, Krista's pale and somewhat haggard, but finally paroled, mother. "Proverbs 31, verses 10 and 11 say, 'When one finds a worthy wife, her value is far beyond pearls. Her husband entrusting his heart to her, has an unfailing prize.'" Mama finished her comments with a tearful smile, speaking to Krista alone. "Welcome, daughter."

Following his strict instructions, Nathan played exactly eight B-side songs that he and Krista had laboriously chosen before he announced, sadly, that the computer had crashed and there would be no more music. "Have a lovely evening and a safe drive home," he said, and started loudly packing his DJ gear. Peter and I had already alerted the Driskill that the happy couple were on their way.

Trixie and Jacky left with a fussy Dah-lee, who Becca had dubbed Dah-ling, and Peter and Mama and I were very shortly left alone to clean up the streamers and vacuum up the rice. "How's your eye, Pete?" Mama asked.

Peter grinned at her. "It's feeling fine, Frances, thank you."

"You know we can't take communion tomorrow. Not until we go to confession," Mama said.

"What do you need to go to confession for, Peter?" I asked. He shrugged.

"Mama?"

"We have all sinned and come short of the glory of God, Eloise," Mama said, and I agreed and turned away. Let them believe they had their little secrets. We all have our little secrets. But I knew that, narcissistic praise-junkies that they were, they wouldn't be able to keep themselves from confessing to me so I could tell them what a worthy performance they'd given.

Made in the USA
Charleston, SC
08 August 2012